The Saga of Silver Bend

THE SAGA
OF SILVER BEND

J. E. GRINSTEAD

The Saga of Silver Bend

Originally published as a 3-part serial in
Argosy All-Story Weekly, March 16, 23, 30 1929.

Published by Wildside Press, LLC.
Visit us online at wildsidepress.com.

CHAPTER I

The Mess in the Bottle

Two riders were hazing a little band of cattle northward on a prairie trail. Half a mile ahead of them the trail dropped over the rimrock into a broad, hazy valley. That valley was known as Silver Bend.

One of the riders was a round-faced little chap, whose high heels helped him to be five feet four. His eyes were the wide, innocent blue eyes of a baby. He might have been twenty or he might have been thirty; his age didn't show. His auburn hair was inclined to curl, and therefore he was called Dolly. He had another name, but nobody in the cow country knew or cared what it was.

The other man was long and lank, flat of cheek, with a pair of cold, keen gray eyes that peered from under bony brows. Eyes that saw things and were thoughtful.

Never were two men less alike, physically and characteristically, than these two. Yet, gaunt, saturnine, thoughtful Old Sankey and the capricious Dolly were side-partners. As he circled a yearling, and drifted back to the side of Sank, Dolly broke into the song of Railroad Ranch:

> *"Hobble the left foot, turn loose the right,*
> *That's about as long as we ever stop at night.*
> *Workin' on the Railroad,*
> *Mighty little pay,*
> *Workin' on the Railroad,*
> *Eatin' prairie hay.*
>
> *"Unroll your blankets and spread 'em on the ground,*
> *Can't get asleep before the boss comes round,*
> *Workin' on the Railroad, up at break of day,*
> *Workin' on the Railroad for mighty little pay."*

1

"Shut up, Dolly," growled Old Sank. "You make my head ache, and, besides that, this ain't no time for singing fool songs."

"How come it ain't?"

"You ask how come? Don't you know we're riding right into the roughest mess since the soap boiled over?"

"What mess?"

"Why, a lot of them killers acrost the river sent word they'd be over to cut the herd, when the Railroad held its home round-up. They ain't huntin' cattle, they're hunting trouble, and they're goin' to find some."

"Uh-huh! Yes, sir, boss! If they jump Old Railroad Ross, they'll be smoke."

The partners drew rein just where the high point of prairie broke over the rimrock into the valley. To right and left they could see the river, almost beneath them, where only a narrow ridge kept the stream from cutting across.

Silver Bend, so called from the silvery cottonwoods that marked the course of the river, lay before them like a map. A great loop, six miles deep and four miles wide at the widest point, with its neck less than a mile across. In the middle distance lay the Railroad Ranch house and pens.

* * * *

"Looks like a dang bottle, don't it, Sank?" said Dolly, musingly.

"It is a bottle, son, and it's got a mess in it that ain't fitten for humans. It's goin' to get shook, and some of the mess is goin' to be took, to-day. Any minute."

"Huh! It ain't happened yet," and Dolly pointed to a cloud of dust that rose, half a mile west of the ranch, in an open prairie valley. "They're still cuttin' 'em."

"It'll happen, all right."

"Then come on. We don't want to miss the party, if there's goin' to be one."

"No, I reckon not, but if you had been to as many parties like that as I have, you wouldn't be in such a rush."

2

"I been to some. What makes you figure on a mess in Silver Bend, anyway?"

"Seen it coming. Recollect I been workin' on the Railroad ten year. You ain't been here but a year, and they's plenty you don't know. Mostly, you've 'hobbled the left foot and turned loose the right.' Not sleeping at night, you been asleep in the daytime. This mess has been brewing for a long time, and now it's about ripe to boil over."

"Well, let her boil. What of it?"

"Plenty. If it was just a ruckus between the Railroad and that Holderness gang across the river it wouldn't be so bad, but if it starts it drags in the Bend and the whole country adjacent. Old Railroad Ross and his three boys are apt to be the center of it, but it'll spread. Railroad will spread it, if it starts."

"I see. Them's the kind of happy settlement I've busted into. I been here a year and ain't heard a gun, except some fellow shootin' at a hawk or a coyote, and now—"

"And now you're apt to hear two guns—or more. But come on. Let's drift 'em on down there."

Down the steep hill and into the timber, they followed the band of cattle. Asa Ross, the eldest of the three Ross boys, and acting foreman, had sent Sank and Dolly out onto the big prairie early that morning to get this bunch off the head of Elm Branch. Old Sankey didn't mention it, but he and Asa Ross had been pretty close, and he suspected Asa had sent him away to keep him out of trouble. They had found the cattle without difficulty and were bringing them in at mid afternoon, instead of at nightfall, as Asa probably expected them to do.

At the edge of the prairie valley the cattle they were driving scented the big round-up herd and scampered on toward it. The partners drew rein at the edge of the prairie. A familiar scene lay before them. The "cutting" was in progress. No rodeo stuff. Just hard-working, skillful riders, on highly trained horses, cutting cattle from an immense herd, while other riders held the herd in place.

3

Everybody who was ever in the cow country has seen a round-up, but this one in Silver Bend was loaded.

On the side of the herd toward them, Sank and Dolly could see a knot of men sitting quietly on their horses, watching the work. They could make out Old Railroad Ross, sitting his horse straight as an Indian, despite his three-score-and-odd years. Suddenly, above the din of bawling cattle, they heard the flat, echoless report of a gun. They saw Old Railroad's gun flash in the sun, as he jerked it from the holster. They saw his horse lunge as the spurs went in, and then they heard a medley of shots, yells, and tramping hoofs.

"Come on!" snapped Sankey, fairly lifting his mouth with his spurs, and darted toward the battle, with Dolly crowding him for the lead.

"Come on!" snapped Sankey, fairly lifting his mouth with his spurs, and darted toward the battle, with Dolly crowding him for the lead.

* * * *

They were too late to see the fight. Such battles are not of long duration. They were not too late to see some of the results of this one, but it would be a long time before all the results were seen.

A few neutrals were trying to hold the big herd and keep it from breaking into a stampede. A small party of men were riding hard for the timber at the north side of the prairie, firing backward as they rode. A dozen riders were in pursuit, pouring volley after volley at the fugitives. Just at the edge of the timber, one of the fugitives threw up his hands and pitched from the saddle.

The pursuers stopped. They were fighters, but canny fighters. They were not going to crowd that gang, when the others were behind trees. They turned back toward the round-up ground and reached it just as Sankey and Dolly did. They were led by Old Railroad Ross himself. He dismounted and stooped over the man who lay on the ground near the herd. It was Asa Ross.

The other men stood back in silence, as the old ranchman's jaws set and quivered with emotion. Asa was dead. A fair-haired, pleasant-faced man of around thirty stepped out of the group and went to Old Railroad's side. This was Peyton Ross, next younger than Asa. There were tears on his cheeks, and he couldn't speak for sobs. The iron had never entered Pate Ross's soul. He couldn't stand rough stuff. Railroad looked at him with a glance of almost contempt, then, ignoring this living son, he turned to the other men and said:

"Get a wagon around here, fellows. Load Asa in and take him to the house. I'll ride on and tell mother."

Ross caught his horse and mounted, then stopped and looked over the men, as if he were counting them.

"Where's Randy, Leck?" he inquired of the leathery old puncher, who stood near.

"I don't know, sir," replied Leck. "He was with the bunch that went after them fellows, and he ain't come back."

"Sank, you and Dolly go find Randy, and bring him home," and Railroad Ross rode grimly away toward his house. He was bereaved of the son upon whom he meant to shift the load in his declining years. Now he was framing what he would say to his good wife, when he reached that rambling old house in the edge of the timber.

Sankey called Old Leck aside and said:

"Leck, you heard what the old man told me to do. The fight was over when we got here. Tell me how it happened, and where I'm apt to find Randy."

"Ain't much to tell about the fight. It come up like most of 'em do, only this one was planned to make it cold murder. Early this morning Bell Holderness and his two brothers, Sam and Steve, comes across to the round-up. With 'em is two fellows I don't know. Some of the gang that hangs out at the Holderness ranch, I reckon. The other man with 'em was Ben Tarleton, and—"

"Ben Tarleton! Are you sure of that?"

"'Course I'm sure. Knowed him all his life. You knew Ben had sorty gone to the wild bunch, didn't you?"

"I knew the grand jury was after him for some of his devilment, but nothin' serious."

"Huh! That's the way they all start. Anyway, six of 'em had been here all day. At noon they et at the chuck wagon, and Old Railroad treated 'em just like he did the rest. A little while ago the six of 'em got together and rode around to the north side of the herd. I thought they was fixing to leave, and was glad of it. But they stopped in a bunch and sat watching Charlie Stone cut, on that little brown bronc of hisn. I reckon everybody was watchin' Charlie except me. I saw Asa Ross go round a steer and turn it back to the herd. As Asa trotted back toward the herd he passed close to the Holderness outfit. I was so far away that I couldn't hear anything that was said, but Asa stopped and the next second there was a shot. Asa never did draw."

"Huh! Cold killin's always start hell in the cow country," commented Sankey. "But what about Randy Ross? Where am I apt to find him?"

"You know where he is as well as I do. Where does he always go when trouble comes up, that he ain't got the nerve to face?"

"You mean—Why, Leck, he couldn't do that, at a time like this! The yellow, unprincipled whelp. Old Man Railroad just had one boy. The other two is women with britches on. Damn Randy's sorry soul, he—"

"Hush! Don't talk so loud. It won't do no good. Old Railroad lies to himself about Randy, and you got to lie to him, no matter what you find, nor where you find it. Better ride now. Better go north until you get out of sight in the woods."

Mounting his horse, Sankey rode north, with Dolly by his side. Neither of them spoke until they reached the edge of the timber, and then they stopped. On the ground lay a handsome, dark young man, dead. He was well clad in garments that had known the hand of an expert tailor. A handsome gold watch chain lay across his vest. His boots were of the finest make. The face was of patrician mold and told of good lineage.

"There's some more hell!" growled Sankey.

"I don't see anything but a dead man," returned Dolly. "I just seen another one back yonder. Looks like a hoss trade to me."

"Hoss trade, hell. Asa Ross was the best cowman, or any other sort of man that ever stretched a stirrup strap. Call it a trade to swap Asa for that carrion?"

"Well," drawled Dolly, "the Railroad might have give some boot. Maybe they throwed Randy Ross in for good measure. Looks like it."

"Damn Randy Ross! He ain't worth thinkin' about. Don't you know who this fellow is?"

"I shore don't. All I know about him is that he's ter'ble dead."

"No, I reckon you don't. He's been away from here the last year. Over in the Indian country, sorty on the dodge."

"I see. He didn't know much about dodgin' or else he didn't know much about Old Railroad Ross. Who is he? Tells me—he won't mind being introduced to a cow-puncher now, even if he has got a pearl-handled gun."

"That's Ben Tarleton."

"Huh! Sounds like something to make a summer dress out of, to me."

"Oh, you dang fool, you don't know anything about Silver Bend and the folks adjacent. Come on and let's find Randy and take him home, like the old man said."

A little way into the timber, Sank turned sharp to his left. They circled the west side of the open prairie, keeping in the timber until they were headed south, following a trail that led up the river.

"Wait a minute, Sank," called Dolly, and when Sankey stopped, "Where are you heading, anyway? If Randy chased them fellows and they got him, he'd be somewhere back toward the ford, on the west side of the Bend."

"Yes, he would, but he didn't. Randy's gone up the river to Willow Mills to drown his troubles. Every time he stubs a toe or a dance gets called off on account of the weather, he's got to get drunk, so's he can stand it."

"Don't be too hard on Randy. He's just—"

"Too hard, nothing. How could I be too hard on a chap that would run away at a time like this? Poor Old Railroad didn't have

7

but one boy. Pate's a good fellow, but he orto been a woman. Randy's just too hell-fired, awful dam' sorry to live. That's what he is. He ain't got as much nerve as—"

"Don't choke yo'self, Sank," drawled Dolly, while a hard, glinting light came into his baby-blue eyes. "Let yo' tongue rest a minute. Yo're talking about me some, and it sorty scratches."

"About you! Why, dang yo' red-haired, fightin' fool soul, you'd rather eat smoke than flapjacks and honey. That's why I tied up with you."

"I know, but—you're talkin' about me just the same. A fellow don't learn to face rough stuff until he has it pushed on him. When I was a kid I used to run off and hide when the family got ready to go to a funeral. I was afraid of dead people. I never got over it until my partner, out at a line-rider's cabin, got busted by a bad bronc. I had to pack him to the shack. I had to wait on him until he bled to death inside. I had to watch him die, and then I had to pack him on a bronc and take him to headquarters. It took that to cure me, and I'd have dodged it if I could. When I was Randy's age, I was just as bad as he is."

"Randy's age? How old are you?"

"Thirty-five, and I been through hell backward, forward, and sidewise. Randy Ross is a thoroughbred. He's got a heart in him as big as a house, and he's got plenty nerve, too. Old Railroad knows it. Charlie Stone forked a bad bronc the other day and rode it ragged. I was standing close to Railroad and I heard him mutter: 'Just like Randy. A thoroughbred ain't worth a damn until it's busted.'"

"Yeah! That goes when they ain't been spoilt, but Randy's spoilt. Plumb ruined. He'll never get busted. Railroad has give him money, got him out'n his scrapes, and laughed at his devilment until nothing can't be did, now."

"Maybe not, but the best bronc I ever rode in my life was a busted outlaw. Men's like horses, they have to be busted. I reckon if you'd look back aways, you'd see where they was some dust and the ground tore up when you got rode."

Old Sankey looked at Dolly with a puzzled expression in his gray eyes. This mess had shown him a new side of his little partner. He had known all along that Dolly had courage, but he had never suspected any depth to him. Dolly had touched a spot in the old puncher that nobody knew about. He, too, had "been rode." It had been a long time ago, but he could remember it.

"All right, Dolly, I'll let my tongue rest; but we got to get on after Randy. He's gone to Willow Mills. Leck seen him when he started. We'll find him drunk. We got to take him home, and we got to lie about where we found him, when we get there. Let's ride."

They rode on up the river trail through the big cottonwoods. As he led the way, Sankey was doing some real thinking and wondering if Dolly could be right. He didn't believe it.

CHAPTER II

Randy Takes the Acid Test

A mile farther on the partners came to where the high point of prairie pushed in to form the stopper to the Silver Bend bottle. Here the river crowded close to the bluff, and the trail ran along the foot of the bluff and close to the high, red banks of the river for a quarter of a mile, with the valley on the other side. Beyond that narrow pass, the bottom broadened again on their side, and formed the considerable community of plantations that supported the better business of the town of Willow Mills. Just before entering this narrow defile, Sankey stopped and said:

"There's two things I want to mention. One is that some time, when the river is high, two sticks of dynamite, one mule, and one bull-tongue plow is all it would take to turn the water across here, cut a new channel, and leave Silver Bend on the other side."

"All of which ain't got nothing to do with finding Randy and getting him back home as quick as possible."

"Maybe not, but here's something that has. A man in them seedling cottonwoods, just across the river, could pick us off easy as we go through that narrow place, and I ain't quite ready to be picked."

"They ain't had time to get up here and get set, but that'll be a good thing to remember. Go ahead."

They rode on through the pass, watching the thicket of young cottonwoods on the other side of the stream. Sankey breathed a sigh of relief as they entered the big bottom above the bend. The river turned back west, and slightly north, here. The trail entered a wide lane that ran due west, two miles, to Willow Mills.

To the south of the lane, left of the riders, a number of farmhouses and broad fields could be seen. On their right, north of the lane, and about a mile from the town, stood a big, two-story white house, with green blinds and trimmings. There was no house near it. A few tenant houses stood well back along the river.

"I been seeing that house ever since I've been in this country," said Dolly, pointing ahead. "Who lives there?"

"Everything to the right of the lane, in this bottom, is the Tarleton plantation. The Tarletons have been here ever since Texas has been Texas. Old Judge Tarleton's grandfather settled the place."

"Judge Tarleton? Anything to that young chap we saw layin' dead in the bushes back a ways?"

"Yes, right smart. Ben Tarleton was the youngest son of Judge Tarleton. That makes this big white house one of the corner posts of the three-cornered mess that starts in Silver Bend to-day, and won't stop until God knows when."

"Just farmers, ain't they?"

"No. They're planters. There's a difference. The people who live in the shacks and work the land are farmers. The old judge is a real, by gad, sir, Southern planter. The kind that reaches for his gun when he's insulted. He's apt as not to take the killin' of Ben as an insult. The judge is pretty old, but he's got two more boys, and ary one of 'em would think it a disgrace to run from the devil if he had a red-hot pitchfork in his hand."

"Nice folks. You said this is a three-cornered mess. Where's the other corner? I might want to run the lines some time—or maybe dodge 'em."

"The other corner is one of the outposts of hell. It's the Holderness ranch, owned by Bell Holderness and his brothers. Steve Holderness married an Indian woman. That gives him a right to hold land in the Indian country. Bell Holderness, the oldest brother and a bachelor, furnishes the brains for the outfit, and everybody knows he owns the ranch in Steve's name. The reason they ain't pirates is because they ain't got a ship."

"Some more nice people. But look! Ain't that Randy Ross?"

* * * *

The sun was just setting behind the distant forest. At the mouth of a broad lane that ran back through an avenue of tall poplars to

11

where the Tarleton home stood in its grove of locust trees, a man and a woman sat their horses, as if they had merely met at that spot and stopped to pass the time of day.

That is exactly what had happened. Neither of them noticed the approach of the two riders. Suddenly, the man whirled his horse in the road and went thundering on toward Willow Mills. The woman put her hand to her brow, to shade her eyes against the glare of the setting sun, and stared after him.

Not until the two punchers were fairly abreast of her did she notice them. With a quick glance at her, as she turned her head, Dolly saw the same patrician feature that had marked the dead face of Ben Tarleton.

"Good evening, Miss Zella," said Sankey, sweeping his hat from his head.

"Oh, Mr. Sankey, I'm so glad it is you," returned Zella Tarleton. "Maybe you can do something with Randy. I—I don't know this gentleman with you, but—"

"You can say anything you like in his presence, ma'am. He'd forget to eat if a lady asked him to forget."

"I'm sure of that, or he wouldn't be with you. I know you haven't any patience with Randy, but he's good. He's just—he's just spoiled and irresponsible, generally, but now he seems to be demented."

"What seems to be the matter with him now?"

"I don't know. I met him here, and he didn't want to stop and talk to me. Something terrible has happened. He said he was going to kill Bell Holderness, and after that, he didn't care what happened. He said that half a dozen times. I begged him to go to the house, and tell me what was wrong, but he was almost insulting, and broke away while I was talking to him."

"That does sound like he was crazy," drawled Sank. "If he wouldn't listen to you he ain't apt to listen to me."

"I know, Mr. Sankey, but you must do something! Get to him before he—You know how he gets when he's in trouble. Get him to go home. Make him go home. He wouldn't have a chance with Bell Holderness."

"Then I reckon we better ride," said Sank, shaking his bridle reins. "I'll do my best, Miss Zella."

"Now who dealt that lady a hand in the game?" asked Dolly when they were out of earshot.

"She deals 'em herself and deals 'em square," snapped Sank. "It's a damn shame for a woman like that to be crazy over a sorry cub like Randy Ross."

"Oh, I see. That brings on more talk. Why don't she marry him and reform him?"

"She's got too much sense to try a fool stunt like that. She's told him plenty of times that she'd marry him whenever he showed her that he could keep straight, and be a man. Every time she tells him that he goes and gets drunk to drown his sorrow."

"I see. Let's go to Willow Mills," and Dolly shot down the road like a flash, with Sank spurring hard to keep up with him.

Willow Mills was but a border village, with half a dozen stores, blacksmith shop, hotel, two saloons, and a dance hall. It was a combination farm center and cow-town, and like all border towns, especially those on the line between Texas and Indian Territory, it was rough. As the partners rode into town they saw Randy dismount in front of the Cottonwood Saloon, and drop his bridle on the ground. They saw him pull his gun from the holster, spin the cylinder, put it back, and then disappear into the saloon.

"If he meets Bell Holderness in that shape, old Railroad Ross loses another boy," snapped Sank. "Come on, let's get him before he gets to drinking."

* * * *

They stepped to the door and looked in. There was no one in the place but Randy and the bartender. Randy Ross was standing in the full light of the big hanging lamp. He was a picture of physical beauty for a man. Full six feet, broad of shoulder, and tapering to the waist. His head was finely modeled, and his features good. He was as well clad as Ben Tarleton had been, and after much the same fashion. His physical strength was such that he showed no more than his twenty-five years, in spite of his dissipation.

13

"Ain't it a damn shame for a man like that to be yellow?" muttered Sankey.

"He ain't yellow, or he wouldn't be here," replied Dolly. "Come on. Let's get him out of there."

"You get him out. He's taken one drink, and the devil couldn't stop him."

Randy had taken one drink, set his glass on the bar, and was reaching for the bottle, when Dolly said, at his elbow:

"Wait a minute, Randy, I want to see you outside."

"Why, hello, Dolly! What are you doing here? Just in time to help me take a drink. Give us another glass, and—"

"No. Sometimes I drink and sometimes I don't."

"This is when I do," returned Randy, and filled his glass to the brim.

Dolly caught his arm, and he looked into those blue eyes, which had gone cold and dark.

"Set that glass down, Randy. If you take another drink right now, you'll curse yourself for it as long as you live. People are saying you are yellow. Let that alone. Come with me, and show 'em you ain't yellow."

Randy set the glass down and turned slowly away from the bar. His face had gone hard and set.

"Show me somebody that says I'm yel—" he began, and then stopped. "Dolly, I am yellow. Yellow as paint. I wish to God I wasn't!"

"No, you're not yellow. Come on outside. I want to talk to you."

For half an hour the two of them squatted in the deep shadow by the blacksmith shop. Old Sankey kept them located by the red glow of their cigarettes, while he watched for the possible coming of Bell Holderness. Dolly talked as he had never talked in his life. At last he said:

"You can't whip anything by running from it. I know; I've tried it. Come on. Let's go back to the ranch. I'll stay with you and help you face it."

The three of them mounted and rode out of town. Preposterous as it might seem, Randy had never touched or looked upon a dead person. For several years there had been no occasion to see such things. Prior to that time he had simply run away from them, and to-day he had done the same thing.

Probably no other man in the Railroad outfit understood Randy's feeling in the matter, except little Dolly. Up to the time he saw Zella Tarleton, Dolly hadn't cared much what happened, but something in the girl's pleading tone had determined him to save Randy from himself. There was going to be trouble, and plenty of it, in Silver Bend, but Randy Ross had to face it like a man, for that girl. At the lane leading to the Tarleton place, Randy stopped.

"Let me go in here a minute, fellows," said Randy. "I'll come on and catch up with you."

He wasn't fooling Dolly. The little puncher knew what would happen. Randy would go back to town and try to drown his troubles. He cudgeled his brain, and finally:

"They might not want you in there, Randy. They might heard about Ben by this time, and—""Ben! What about Ben?"

"Didn't you know he was killed in that mess at the Railroad to-day?"

"Killed! My God, no!"

"Yes, he was killed. I saw him."

"Then I don't want to go in there. Let me go back to town."

"No," said Dolly, firmly. "We're going back to the Railroad. That's the best place for all of us right now."

They rode on through the lane and struck the trail that ran through the narrows. Sank led the way, then came Randy, and Dolly brought up the rear. He was back there because he didn't mean to let Randy Ross turn and get away from him.

He knew that terrible thing that was gripping Randy's heart with icy fingers. It wasn't fear. It was a tangible thing, worse than fear. He himself had lain awake at night, gripped by it. It couldn't be tamed. It had to be killed, and only one thing could kill it. That was contact with the dead.

Just as they reached the narrows, two shots rang on the night, and a minute later two riderless horses came bounding along the trail toward them. They stopped the horses, and old Sank felt over the saddles in the darkness.

"One of 'em's Leck's and the other Pate's," he said.

"Well, let's get down the trail," said Dolly. "Whoever done it has run away, and maybe the boys are just shot up a little."

He knew better, but they pushed on, the two riderless horses trotting ahead of them, with bridles over the saddle horns. At the narrowest place, the lead horse snorted, shied, and the two of them whirled and came back to the riders.

"I'll—I'll hold the horses while you look," said Randy.

"No, come on," insisted Dolly. "The horses will stand."

Randy dismounted and staggered along the trail. Fifty yards farther on, they found Leck, stone dead. Twenty feet beyond him lay Peyton Ross.

"I'll—I'll get the horses," faltered Randy.

"No. Let Sank bring them."

They stood together, within a few feet of Leck's body, until the horses came. Dolly knew, only too well, what Randy was suffering. He recalled that night in a line-rider's cabin, with his dead partner. This was the baptism of death for Randy. He'd either come out of it a brave man or a hopeless coward, according to the stuff that was in him.

"Hold the horse, Sank," commanded the little puncher. "You take his shoulders, Randy. You're stronger than me."

How Randolph Ross went through that ordeal he never knew. When Leck was lashed to his horse, they went on to Peyton Ross. As they lifted the body to its saddle, sobs were shaking Randy, but they were no longer sobs of fear and dread. He loved this gentle, kindly brother, as if he were a sister. He had always stood in awe of Asa, who was ten years his senior, and paid little attention to him.

Suddenly Randy laid his hand on his brother as he lay bound to the saddle, and in a husky tone that seemed the very tearing of his heartstrings, he said:

16

"Good-by, Pate. You'll go to God, if ever man did. I won't forget you, and I won't forget the men that done this." He was cold now, and when he spoke a moment later, his voice was hard and even. "Each one of you boys lead one of the horses. You won't have to watch me now, Dolly. I'll lead the way, so if those fellows are still in the brush, you'll get a warning."

"God! What a dose for a man to take," whispered Dolly to the silent old Sankey, as Randy mounted, and rode on down the trail. "He took it like a man, too. Don't tell me he's yellow!"

* * * *

A light was burning in the house at the Railroad Ranch, while some of the men sat up with the dead, as was the custom of the country. A light also showed in the long bunk house.

There would be little sleeping that night. The men talked among themselves in low tones. Asa Ross, as foreman of the ranch, had been a hard driver, but fair, and the men liked him. They wondered who would handle the men now.

For all of old Railroad's dash that day in the gun fight, they knew he was too old for the job. Peyton couldn't do it. He was too tender-hearted. He'd either give the ranch away, or somebody would take it away from him. There was no use to consider Randy. He was too young, and besides that, he was yellow, and a drinker. All these things the men talked over among themselves.

The evening was chilly, and old Railroad Ross sat by a little fire in the open fireplace. Asa's body was in another room. Railroad was alone with his grief. The grief of such men is not normal. They feel as deeply, perhaps, as other people, but their grief seems to benumb and harden them. Often such men are charged with looking upon death as merely a physical loss.

Ross had been disappointed in the matter of sons. He wanted a houseful of them; ten had been born to him. As one man put it, owing to rattlesnakes, round-up fights, and rough stuff, only three reached full manhood. Asa was now gone. Peyton was also gone, but the old fellow didn't know it as he sat staring, hard-eyed, at the

17

fire, and trying to get his bearings in this storm that had overtaken him as he neared the last port on the seas of life.

Silver Bend, all of it, twelve thousand acres in extent, had been acquired by Ross in his early manhood. His real name was Randolph Ross. His brand was plain RR. He said he knew the brand could be run, but that a thief would take your stuff anyway, if you didn't watch it.

Waggish cowboys dubbed the place Railroad Ranch. From that it was but a step to calling the ranchman Railroad Ross. As the years passed he became so known all over the far-flung ranges. Even the banks thought that the initial in his signature, "R. Ross," stood for Railroad.

Railroad cattle and horses in thousands roamed the unfenced prairies to the southward, but Silver Bend was Railroad's home, and he loved it in the peculiar way that such men love their homes.

He was wondering now who would carry on, and keep it together, when he was gone. Of all his boys, Randy, the baby, named for his father and more like his sire in some ways than any of the others, had been the bitter disappointment. What would the spoiled, irresponsible Randy do with Silver Bend and the Railroad if it fell to him? The old man's musings were interrupted by low voices and shuffling steps at the side gate of the yard, heard through the open door.

He stepped out into the yard and called:

"What is it, boys?"

"Come out here, please, Mr. Ross," replied Sank, and then when he reached them the old puncher went on in low tones:

"It's Pate and Leck. We found 'em up at the narrows."

"Found 'em? What do you mean? Dead?"

"Yes, sir. I reckon somebody got the water light on 'em from across the river and just potted 'em."

"Potted Pate. Murdered him. He never done a thing to anybody in his life. Him and Leck was goin' to town to get a coffin for Asa and have a grave dug. Pate didn't even have a gun on him. And they just bushed him, cold."

The old man's voice was hard and hummed like a taut wire. He stopped and seemed to be trying to control himself before those strained wires broke. Presently he went on in a flat, lifeless tone:

"Take Pate in the room where Asa is and lay him out. Better take Leck to the bunk house, I reckon. He'd feel more at home there."

He turned away and took a few steps, and then turned back. "I sent you after Randy, Sank. Did you find him?"

"Here I am, dad," said Randy, stepping forward from the group by the gate.

"Come on in the house. The other boys can attend to things out here."

He and his one remaining son went into the house together. What terrible thoughts of havoc and disaster were in the mind of old Railroad Ross at that moment none would ever know.

CHAPTER III

The Vigil at Railroad Ranch

Railroad and Randy sat down by the fire. The old man threw on a fresh stick of wood, filled his pipe, lit it, and smoked in silence. The clock ticked mournfully on the mantel. There was no sound about the house except an occasional low-spoken word, or a light step on tiptoes. The whole place seemed to be in silent mourning. It was so still in that room that a bit of falling ember in the fire could be heard.

At last Railroad spoke:

"Randy, it looks like the old Railroad is square up ag'in' its last fight, and mighty shorthanded for such a bad mess. Asa's gone, and I'm too old to carry on. I been wondering about you. I ain't never pulled the hackamore on you like I ought to, I reckon. I didn't have much fun when I was a boy. By the time you grew up I had right smart money, and I just turned you loose. You ain't never been rode none, Randy, and you've sorty gone bronc on me, but, Randy—Boy, I—I need a man right now."

Old Railroad choked and stopped. For the first time since he had stood over Asa as he lay on the ground, the old fellow broke and a tear glistened on his flat, hard cheek.

Followed minutes of silence. The clock ticked on. The two men, startlingly alike except in age, sat staring into the fire, the red light on their bronze faces.

Finally Randy stirred in his chair, cleared his throat, and said:

"Dad, I'm—I'm going to try to be a man."

Railroad turned his head and stared at Randy, as if one of his dead sons had spoken to him, but said no word, and Randy went on:

"I've been a worthless, drunken pup, dad, and, worst of all, I've been yellow as paint."

"No! Not yellow!"

"Yes, dad, yellow. I'm coming clean. Sank and Dolly would lie to you about me, just as everybody else has done, but I'm going to tell you the truth. When I saw Asa dead I didn't have the nerve to face it. I ran away. I went to Willow Mills to get drunk and forget it, like the yellow pup I was. That's where they found me. Don't let them tell you anything else."

"Go on," commanded Railroad. "It's hard as hell to take, but give me the whole dose."

"The rest won't be so hard to take, dad. Little Dolly got me out of the Cottonwood some way. I think he must have done it with his eyes. Then he talked to me. He made me come home. He watched me, and when I tried to turn back and run away from it he wouldn't let me."

"God made a man when he made Dolly. If He'd made him any bigger, he'd be the biggest man in the world. It's bitter, but I can take it. Go on."

"When we found Leck and Pate I tried to run away again. Dolly made me help him put them on the horses. Dad, it wasn't live men I was afraid of. It was dead men and death itself. I never told you before, because I was ashamed of it. I'm telling you now because I'm cured of it."

"What!"

"Yes, cured. When I put my hand on Pate all the yellow went out of me. He never was afraid; he just didn't want to hurt anybody. From that moment on I wasn't afraid of anything, and I never will be again. All I want now is a chance to prove it, and square things for the cold killing of Asa and Pate."

"Thank God!" said Railroad in a husky voice as he gripped the hand of his one remaining son. "You're giving me help when I need it. I didn't see how I was going to get by this, but I can now."

Randy rose and left the room. Railroad didn't know where he was going. Perhaps out to the bucket that hung on a hook on the long black gallery, to get a drink.

Randy went into the room where his two murdered brothers lay. He turned back the sheets and looked at them. No one in the room spoke a word. They stared at Randy and wondered. They noticed something that Randy himself had not noticed. His long Colt .45 was still in the holster at his belt.

Some of the grim old punchers took it as an omen, others looked upon it as they would have looked upon wearing a hat in the presence of the dead.

* * * *

Randy replaced the sheets gently, turned, and left the room. He had faced the dead without a quiver. He could face anything now. Returning, he sat down in the chair by his father.

"Dad, I don't know where nor how to begin, but I'm ready to try to be a man. Tell me what to do, and I'll do my best. I don't understand why we are in this trouble. I don't understand why the Holderness boys—"

"Just a minute, Randy. You would not understand it. It's old, old trouble that began when you was a baby. Twenty-four year ago this round-up time. Sam Holderness, the daddy of these Holderness boys, ranched in above Willow Mills. Sam was a blustering sort of fellow and didn't amount to much, but right self-important. At the round-up that spring Sam and me had an argument over some brands.

"I don't know what anybody else said to Sam, or whether they egged him on. All I know is that along late in the afternoon Sam came at me, makin' smoke. I was right handy with a gun in them days; had to be. I shot Sam.

"The bullet went through his right lung and stopped him, but didn't kill him. He got up all right, but come winter he took pneumonia and died. I don't know whether that bullet hole in his lung had anything to do with it or not. Some of the doctors said it did, and others said it didn't; but no matter. There was plenty of busy-bodies to say that I killed Sam Holderness.

"I felt bad about it, of course. Sam didn't have anything much, and he had left a widow and three little boys. Bell was about ten year old then. A quiet, say-nothing boy. The youngest one wasn't more than a baby. I went to the administrator of Sam's estate and put ten thousand dollars where he could draw on it for the widow and children, without anybody knowing where it come from."

"They made out all right. The boys grew up. Sam's widow married and went away from this country; but the boys stayed. They worked with cattle. I knew 'em all, and they seemed to treat me same as anybody else.

"Then two, three year ago Steve Holderness married into the Chickasaw tribe, across the river. Bell had got some money together, trading here and yonder, and they started the Holderness ranch. I thought the old trouble was all forgot, but one day Steve got drunk at Willow Mills and give it out that I was goin' to pay for killin' his daddy.

"There was right smart talk about it here and yonder, but it died down. Then this thing broke to-day, right out of a clear sky. Ain't no doubt but what Bell Holderness has kept this in his gizzard all these years. If they'd killed me, it wouldn't look so bad, but seems like they aim to get my boys one at a time and leave me to suffer out my old age. I thought the country had got civilized some, and we had got away from them old wars, but I was wrong."

"I never heard of that before, dad. I could understand the Holderness boys wanting to meet you and shoot it out, if they thought you killed their father. But this cold killing and bushwhacking of innocent men don't go."

"No, it oughtn't to go; but it looks like they're makin' it go. I understand the Holderness boys are rough. I've never been to their ranch, but I understand it's a sort of hangout for a hard gang of fellows that's dodging the law. That reminds me of Ben Tarleton. What in the kingdom ever made a boy, raised like Ben was, take up with fellows like them?"

"That's the bitterest part of it all, Ben getting killed at our round-up the way he did."

"Well, he was with them fellows. They killed Asa, and one of them got killed. It just happened to be Ben."

"I know, dad, but—you know about Zella and me. She's the only thing that has kept me from going plumb to the devil and being as bad as Ben was."

"Huh! Maybe so, but I got an idea it's partly what's inside of you. I knew you and Zella were sweethearts, and I supposed you'd marry as soon as you got yo' crop of wild oats harvested, but now—"

"Now!" Randy almost gasped. "You wouldn't object to me marrying Zella, because of this?"

"Oh, no. I ain't got a thing ag'in' Zella. She's one of the finest young women in Texas. Trouble is, old Judge Tarleton and them other two boys of hisn, Lav and Cliff, are pretty apt to object some. You look at it from yo' relation to Zella, and it looks bad enough. Look at it from the viewpoint of having the Tarletons join the Holderness gang ag'in' us, and it looks a lot worse."

"I hadn't thought of that."

* * * *

"You better think of it if you're goin' to try to work out of this mess alive. It'll be plain enough that Ben was shot in the back. You couldn't convince the old judge and his boys that ary Tarleton that ever lived would turn his back to an enemy. That leaves it just plain assassination in their minds. Besides that, Ben had not fired a shot. Every chamber of that pearl-handled gun was full."

"Do they know all that?"

"I reckon they do, by this time. Dave Simms was here with the D Bar outfit. They put Ben in their chuck wagon and took him over the prairie road and around that way. Judge Tarleton and the boys may see sense, knowing as they do how Ben's run wild lately. The chances are, though, that they'll go clean crazy. They're good folks, but they can't believe a Tarleton is ever wrong."

"They're the kind that can be awful hard, when they are hard," said Randy, musingly.

"Yes, and they're apt to be hard now. They's one thing. Whatever they do will be done in the open. They won't pot nobody from the bushes. Old Judge Tarleton is likely to just straddle a horse and come storming right over here."

"Dad, it's going to be hard for me," sighed Randy. "If I'd been a man all along, I'd know how to act, but now—"

"Them's things a fellow has to learn by himself. 'Bout all I can tell you is to keep yo' head cool. It don't take a very brave man to kill somebody. It takes a lot braver one to not kill when he's crowded and has a chance to kill. We can handle the Holderness gang if the Tarletons stay out of it. If they don't? Well, let's not cross any bridges before they're built." Lighting his pipe, old Railroad smoked in silence, while Randy pondered his situation.

The following day was a day of funerals at Willow Mills. Members of two of the most prominent families on that part of the border were buried in the same cemetery. The people of the community were in attendance, but the wise ones were tight-lipped. The trouble between Railroad Ross and Sam Holderness was recalled by old men, and they wagged their heads over it.

Few knew any of the facts about the killing of Asa Ross and Ben Tarleton at the Railroad round-up. Randy Ross, Dolly and Sank, and old Railroad knew of the bushwhacking of Pate and Leck, but they had told nothing.

The cortege that came in from the Railroad ranch was ominous. A wagon brought three caskets. Ahead of the wagon rode ten armed men, with Randy Ross in the leading pair, and Dolly by his side. Behind the wagon came the family carriage and a few other vehicles, followed by ten more armed men.

There was pretty likely to be peace until the funeral was over, or a lot more graves would be needed. The procession filed through the wide gate and stopped. At the grave the armed punchers stood about in groups, bare-headed but vigilant.

The Tarleton funeral had entered the gate a few minutes ahead of them. The graves were less than a hundred feet apart. With bowed gray heads, Railroad Ross and the venerable Judge Tarleton stood with their backs to each other, listening to the last rites of their sons.

Randy, outwardly cold but inwardly torn with emotion, stood by his mother's chair. He quivered as his ear caught a few words of what the minister was saying at Ben Tarleton's grave. Among them were, "stricken down in the bloom of youth by an assassin's bullet." That told him how the Tarletons had taken Ben's death, and what he might expect from them in his hour of trouble.

He glanced toward that other funeral, and saw Zella sobbing in the arms of a neighboring woman, and his heart almost broke, because he could not even offer a word of comfort to this woman, who he had loved from his boyhood and who needed him now as he needed her.

* * * *

There was no disturbance at the cemetery. Randy had expected none; but on the return to the ranch every bend of the road, every thicket by the way, was a potential ambush.

He was head of the Railroad outfit now. Old Railroad Ross and his wife got into their carriage when the funeral was over, and waited deferentially for the Tarleton carriage to pass out ahead of them. In it were the judge and his wife, Zella and her two brothers.

There was little show of emotion. Railroad and his wife were silent because they had seen so much sorrow and knew the futility of violent grief. The Tarletons were silent, because violent emotion was unbecoming their patrician blood and lineage. No one in the Tarleton carriage looked toward the Ross equipage.

Passing out the gate, the Tarletons went on toward the white house in the locust grove, followed by no one. Outside the gate, the Railroad outfit formed again, as it had come, and followed at a respectful distance. Two old men stood at the cemetery gate talking, as the crowd broke up and left.

"I never noticed Randy Ross lookin' so much like his daddy before," said one.

"Looks just like Railroad did twenty or thirty year ago," replied the other, "but he won't never be the man his daddy is, if he lives—and he won't."

"Say he won't? Why?"

"I picked up a smatterin' of how this mess comes up. The real quarrel is with the Holderness boys, over the killin' of old Sam years

26

ago. Worst thing Randy's up ag'in', though, is the Tarleton boys. They ain't afraid and they mean business."

"Well, it ain't my quarrel. The less outsiders say about a mess like this, the less they're likely to have to swallow."

"That's right. I wouldn't mention it, except to a fellow like you. It's their quarrel. Hands off and let 'em settle it, I say."

In those few words the sentiment of the better element of the community was expressed, and they would studiously refrain from talking; but there were plenty of irresponsible people who would take sides and let their tongues wag.

Nothing befell the Railroad outfit on the return trip to the ranch. Things were set as nearly to rights as they could be after such a catastrophe. The men went about the late evening ranch work, getting ready for the next day's handling of stock, branding, and the like. Old Railroad and Randy kept to the house. Sank and Dolly went out to round up the remuda.

* * * *

"Dolly," said Sankey, "I got an idea that you've elected yo'self to a right dangerous place."

"Anybody that sticks to the old Railroad now is in a dangerous place, and anybody that quits it is a yeller-bellied hound."

"That may be true, and I reckon it is; but I don't aim to quit, so you ain't hurt my feelings none. Point is, Randy Ross aims to ride, and ride hell-bent for trouble. The Railroad riders will have to go in pairs or better, and somebody's got to ride with Randy. After what happened last night, he's apt to take you."

"Well, I'd hate to leave you, but if he calls me, I'll have to ante."

"Yes, I know you will. Trouble is, whoever rides with Randy is due for about what Leck got for riding with Pate. That Holderness gang aims to clean up on the Railroad and do it quick."

"Looks like it, but unless I miss my measure of Randy, he'll be at the cleaning."

"With the Holderness gang, yes. With the Tarletons, he can't turn a hand."

"Why can't he?"

"Account of Zella."

"Huh! You may see it that way, but I don't. I can see how a man could love that girl to death, but I can't see why he should stand still and let her folks shoot him to shoestrings on account of it, and I don't believe Randy can. Anyway, I ain't in love with her, and if I happen to be between them and Randy, or can get between 'em—"

"Steady! Wait till it happens, to talk about it, and then don't talk. Whatever way things jump, you and me will work together, and we'll find plenty to do before this thing is over. I'm just a pore old puncher, and Randy Ross is the only heir to the Railroad and about a million bronchos and cattle, and has got a fighting chance for the finest girl in Texas, but I wouldn't trade places with him for a whole lot to boot."

The Railroad was quiet enough that night. The men were catching up with their sleep. No one was likely to attack the place, when thirty hard riders and straight shooters were known to be there. But Randy's troubles were not far off.

Came morning, and true to Sankey's prediction, Randy called Dolly to ride with him, but he arranged for Sankey and another trusted old puncher, Con Bates, to be always on the same part of the range with them. They had just saddled up and were ready to ride.

Old Railroad Ross was giving Randy some instructions about the work, when they heard a lone horseman coming up the trail. They turned and saw that the gaunt, stiff man astride the powerful horse was Judge Tarleton!

CHAPTER IV

"Assassinated, Sir. Assassinated!"

A tableau of stoicism was presented as Judge Tarleton rode up and stopped. The old planter had a gun on his hip. Railroad Ross stood like a block of granite, looking square at the visitor. Randy stood by his father's side. Both were armed, but no hostile gesture was made.

The young man's lips were drawn in a hard line. He knew that the Tarleton family had merely tolerated him as Zella's suitor, because she was the only daughter of the house, and usually had her way. His standing there, his hope of winning Zella had long hung by a slender thread.

What was Judge Tarleton's purpose? Would what the old planter had to say sever that thread? Worse still, would it sever the friendly relations between the two old families? He was not left long in doubt.

"Good morning, judge," greeted Railroad. "Won't you get down and come in?"

"No, sir, I won't get down," returned the judge, ignoring the greeting. "I won't go into your house now, and I don't know that I ever shall. I came over here to get some information about the murder of my son."

As he sat there on his horse, Judge Tarleton was the personification of family pride and resentment against a world in which any untoward thing could happen to a Tarleton. Railroad stood calmly looking his neighbor over, from his gray head crowned by a broad black hat, to his fine morocco-topped boots.

Tarleton's cheeks glistened from a fresh shave. He shaved from his temples to a line running from the mustache back to the hinge of the jaw, and he shaved it every day. Below that line was a neatly trimmed beard that had once been black.

The high-bridged nose and other outstanding features that marked Zella and Ben were there. His very air and bearing bespoke the patrician. It said plainly that he didn't know and he didn't care a hang whether he was going to meet with hostility at the Railroad or not. When Ross didn't speak, he rapped out:

"Well, what have you got to say?" much as if the old ranchman had been a slave.

Railroad's face was as fixed as granite, and one expected it to break if he opened his mouth.

"I have to say that murder is a pretty hard word to use about that killing."

"That's what it was. Assassinated, sir, assassinated! I know my people. No Tarleton ever turned his back in a fight. Ben was murdered. Shot in the back by a cowardly assassin."

"That's pretty hard talk, judge. I don't think Ben was assassinated, because there ain't any assassins in my outfit. I wish you could see yo' way to change that word to something else."

"I'll change nothing! The boy was shot in the back. He wasn't fighting. His gun was still in the holster and hadn't been fired. I don't charge you with murder. I've known you a long time. You're rough, but I've found you square. All I want is for you to tell me who killed Ben. My sons and I will attend to the rest."

The tableau turned now. Railroad's lips were a grim line. Finally, he spoke:

"I'm sorry, judge, but I don't know. You haven't asked me how this mess came up, but I'm going to tell you. Bell Holderness and his gang comes here to make trouble and they made it. They killed one of my boys cold. Naturally, I and my men opened on 'em, and they run. I ain't charging nothing against Ben. He was with the Holderness boys and when they ran, he did, and he was killed. Who killed him, I can't say. Several of us were shooting. They were a good distance from us, their horses were running, and ours were running. Whoever killed him was shooting at the crowd and happened to hit Ben."

"So, as near as you can come to it, your outfit murdered Ben?" and Tarleton's lips curled in a silent snarl.

"No, I don't put it that way. Ben was a wild boy. He got in bad company, and somebody in my outfit shot him. I'm sorry, for I don't think Ben had anything against me or the Railroad outfit."

"You admit the killing then! To me and my boys it was murder, and we have our own way of settling with murderers, whether it is one or a hundred. Lav and Cliff wanted to come with me, but I told them no. If you was friendly, and could explain and help us get the murderer, I could do more alone. If you wasn't friendly, I was enough to be shot in the back."

"That's more hard talk, judge," pleaded Railroad. "I, nor ary man in my outfit, ain't got a thing ag'in' you and your boys. Not one of us had anything ag'in' Ben. I've got trouble enough with the Holderness boys 'thout quarrelling with a family that's been friendly and my neighbors for years."

"Never mind that," snapped Tarleton. "I don't feel any blame for being friendly to you. Sometimes it takes a good many years to find people out." Then the judge shifted his glance to Randy's set face. "You have been treated as a friend and an equal at my house, young man. That's past. If you come there again, you come as one of the assassins of my son, and will be treated accordingly."

Randy winced, but didn't speak. He couldn't trust himself. Anyway, Railroad didn't give him a chance.

"Judge Tarleton," he said, as his brows knit, "you've made yourself pretty plain, and I don't know that talking more could do any good. If any trouble comes up between your family and my outfit, you'll have to start it."

"It's already up, sir!" and Tarleton whirled his horse and rode away.

"Too bad!" said Railroad to his son.

"Yes, it is too bad," admitted Randy, "but if nothing else will do them—"

"Wait a minute, Randy. I want to say a word to all of you. Judge Tarleton and his boys are good men—among the best in the country. I want every one of you to keep out of trouble with them if you possibly can without running from them. Mount and ride now, but keep your eyes open."

Without a word, Randy mounted and rode away, with Dolly by his side, and Sank and Con following at a little distance. They were heading toward the round-up grounds. Randy wasn't going to wait for a further demonstration from the Holderness gang. He was going to see what he could find along the river, where Leck and Pate had been killed.

When they reached the round-up ground, they saw Judge Tarleton look back, as he entered the timber on the trail that led up the river. He wasn't a half mile ahead of them, and was riding slowly, apparently to show that he wasn't afraid.

They rode on, entered the timber, and followed on up the trail. When a quarter of a mile from the narrows, they heard a single shot.

"Good God! They've shot the judge!" gasped Randy, and galloped on up the trail, with Dolly at his heels.

* * * *

Coming out on the river bank, where they could see far ahead, they saw a horseman, sagging in his saddle and clinging desperately to the saddle horn. They knew it was Judge Tarleton, but as Randy quickened his speed to go to the old planter's assistance, a gun cracked across the river. Randy's horse reared and crashed to the earth. He rolled free and came up behind a big cottonwood tree.

Dolly spurred his horse behind a thicket, dismounted and crept to the river bank. Something moved in the thicket on the other side of the stream. Dolly's carbine cracked, and a terrible yell came from the thicket. After that, silence.

"I don't know whether you ought to have done that or not, Dolly," said Randy. "You didn't see the man that shot at me, and you might shoot the wrong man."

Dolly looked at him with an odd glint in his blue eyes.

"See here now, Randy. Let's you and me get this straight before we go any further. Do we let that Holderness gang pot us, or don't we? If we're going to fight back, I'll stay with you. If we're going to be potted, why, I ain't ready to be potted, that's all."

"Oh, I mean to fight back and fight hard. I just want it to be in the open."

"Well, it won't be. That gang aims to bushwhack us. Do you know what that fellow's done for you?"

"Why, no, except that he missed me, hit my horse, and left me afoot."

"He's done a heap more than that. He's shot old Judge Tarleton, and the Tarleton boys will lay it on the Railroad outfit. The judge saw us following him, and if he gets home alive, which he probably will, he'll tell 'em it was us."

"Then let me have your horse, and I'll go on and catch up with the judge and tell him better."

"Yes, and he'd believe you, just like you'd believe the biggest liar you ever saw in your life. Now you listen to me. You got to do something more than just not be afraid. You got to use your head in this mess. I been thinking. The Holderness gang ain't just trying to square a mess that happened a hundred years ago. I don't know what they're after, but it's something else. Had you thought of what a hell of a long shot for a six-shooter it was from the Railroad outfit to where that gang went into the woods and Ben Tarleton fell?"

"Why, no. What of it?"

"Well, when Sank and me was out after the remuda yesterday evening, we met Con. He showed us where Mr. Ross and the boys turned back and it's full two hundred yards from there to where Ben fell!"

"I don't see—"

"I don't either, but I'm guessing. I don't believe anybody hit Ben that far with a six-shooter. I believe Bell Holderness shot Ben in the back, as they ran away."

"Bell did! Why would Bell kill one of his own gang?"

"Ben didn't exactly belong. He wasn't that sort. Couldn't be. He probably didn't know what the Holderness boys were up to when they went to the round-up. Maybe he said something about the killing of Asa. It might be, and likely was, that Bell simply figured that if Ben was killed at your round-up, it would put the Tarletons against you, instead of against them, as they would have been if Ben hadn't been killed."

"Dolly, do you suppose—"

"Yes, I suppose a whole lot of things; and among 'em, I suppose we better get your saddle off'n that dead broncho and get away from here."

* * * *

Sank and Con had heard the shots, but misjudged the direction. They came up just as Randy was ready to mount behind Dolly for the return to the ranch. They all returned to the edge of the prairie. Dolly brought a fresh mount for Randy, and then they went into a general discussion of the situation.

Con Bates had been with the Railroad as far back as Randy could remember. He was a typical leather face, and talked so little that people often wondered if he was dumb. He sat on his heels, listening, as the others talked. He heard Dolly's suggestion as to Bell Holderness having shot Ben. He listened to everything and said nothing. Finally, Randy turned to him.

"Con, you've been in many a mess like this. What do you think is the best way to handle it?"

"I been in plenty of messes," growled the wrinkled old puncher, "but none like this. They ain't no two alike. Besides that, I've never been in one when Bell Holderness was ramrodding the other side of the fight."

"A fight's a fight, ain't it?"

"Yes. Sometimes it's a dozen. This is apt to be that kind before it's over. I've known Bell Holderness all his life. He never made a horse trade in his life that he didn't plan every move in it before he said a word. When he brought his gang over here and killed Asa, he had all his plans made. He knows now that Asa and Pate are out of the way. He knows Railroad is too old to push the fight, and he thinks right now that he knows what you'll do."

"I guess he's mistaken about that," said Randy, with a wintry smile, "for I don't know myself."

"Maybe not, but you ain't done what he thought you would, and I don't believe you will."

"What was that?"

"He thought you'd go to Willow Mills and get drunk, and he'd pick a quarrel with you and kill you. Likely he still thinks so."

Randy shot a glance at Dolly, and then:

"He'll miss his guess, if he does. I may go to Willow Mills, but if Bell, or anybody else kills me, he'll kill me sober, and I'll be at the killing."

They rode south, up the hill, and out onto the prairie. The four of them were not together all the time. When noon came, Randy and Dolly stopped under a lone hackberry tree, where they could see a considerable distance in every direction. They took the lunch from their saddle pockets and ate it. Randy was silent and thoughtful. At last he spoke:

"Dolly, you look like a boy, but I know you're a lot older than I am. Anyway, you've been a man longer, for I never was a man until you pulled me out of the Cottonwood and made a man of me. I need help badly. We can't just sit still until they push us over."

"No, I reckon not," grinned Dolly, "but I got a picture of the one that pushes you over while you're still alive. You're so damn fightin' mad right now, Randy, that yore boots are scorching, and you don't know what's the matter with you. Way I look at it is this. Holderness is ahead of the game. He's got three of the Railroad outfit. He's got Ben Tarleton dead and the old judge shot, and got it all laid on us."

"I've proved to myself that I'm not afraid, Dolly, and now I'm ready for anything. If I could just see a place where we could strike, and strike hard, I'm rearing to break Bell's luck. You're right about me being mad."

They rode on back toward the ranch late in the afternoon. They were within half a mile of where Sank and Dolly hazed the band of cattle over the rimrock the day of the round-up, when they saw two riders, each leading a horse, coming in from the west.

"Why, that's Cub and Shorty. I wonder—" and Randy stopped.

"Them two and Keech and Brazos Jim went to town after the mail. I heard Mr. Ross tell 'em to go and for four of 'em to go together."

"Another mistake," said Randy, musingly. "Looked like a dare."

"Looks to me like somebody taken it up. Let's see what they got to say. What's happened, Shorty?"

"Nothing much," drawled the tallest puncher in the outfit, who had been dubbed Shorty. "We rides into town a little after noon. Cub and me goes to the post office, and Keech and Brazos went over to the Cottonwood to wait for us. When we got to the Cottonwood, Keech was layin' on the floor dead, and Brazos, he was down and bleedin'.

"As we stepped in to the place two guns went into our faces, and we was kindly invited to reach for the sky. We reached. Behind one of them guns was Lav Tarleton, and behind the other was Bell Holderness."

"No!"

"Yes, and a right smart of it. Then we got some news. We found out that the whole Railroad outfit confessed to murder. We found out just what we were. We found out that you, Randy, shot old Judge Tarleton in the back. Then we got turned loose, without our guns, to bring the glad tidings that unless Railroad—I mean Mr. Ross—would give up Randy and the man that kilt Ben, they was goin' to be war."

"'Bout thirty days late with that news," said Dolly. "Everybody that ain't blind or crazy, knew it all."

"What did they kill Keech and Brazos for?" asked Randy.

"Not a thing in the world. Keech killed one of Bell's gang, and Brazos two. That was all. We heard the shooting, and thought it was just in fun—but it wasn't."

"Where did Bell and Lav go?" asked Randy.

"They shooed us down the lane as far as the big house. Then they turned us loose to drift, and they went in the house."

"In the house! Bell Holderness went in Tarleton's house?"

It was what Holderness had been trying to get the right to do, ever since Zella became grown. Randy's world was falling about his ears.

CHAPTER V

Ambush

Somebody had been watching Randy and Dolly from a safe place, as they rode across the prairie, but he hadn't watched long enough. The spy didn't see Cub and Shorty, and he didn't see Sank and Con, who were riding down another draw, and coming into Silver Bend a quarter of a mile east of where the trail went down the hill.

Randy led down the trail. His mind was in turmoil. The Railroad and its troubles were of course, the main problem; but what was making those troubles? Was it possible that Bell Holderness had started all this death and destruction in order to get him out of the way? Not likely. If Bell wanted him killed, it would be easy enough to have had some of the Holderness gang pot him from the brush long ago. Zella might be one of the pawns in the game, but certainly not the only one, perhaps not the main one. What was it all about? The only answer he got was the crack of a gun and a whistling bullet that narrowly missed him.

They were well down into the open timber of the bend by this time. The shot had come from his left. Randy didn't look to see where the others of his party were, though he knew that Dolly was a little way behind him.

He whirled his horse into the woods as he drew his gun. He had gone berserk. The blood of a hundred pioneer ancestors was burning in his veins, and all thought of fear or caution was forgotten. His only thought was to mix smoke with the man who had shot at him.

He glimpsed two riders in the woods and opened on them. They returned his fire for a moment. Bullets whistled and leaves and twigs fell around Randy, but he pushed on. Into the mêlée came Dolly, and close behind him Cub and Shorty. Still the attackers stood their ground. There must be quite a party of them. It was growing dusky in the woods. Apparently, no hits were scored on either side. Con and Sank heard the shots and came hurrying on. It sounded like a major battle going on as they came up.

"Come on, fellers!" called Randy. "Let's take 'em," and he spurred straight for the group of trees behind which the enemy had taken shelter. Dolly went with him. Con and Sank sought the flank on one side, while Cub and Shorty took the other.

This was something more than members of the Holderness gang cared to face. They had thought they were going to surprise Randy and the little puncher. Instead, they had jumped six men, none of whom was frightened about being surprised.

The Holderness outfit still had an even break, for there were six of them, but they were not seeking an even break. They gave back for a better position, and made a mistake. Bullets flew among them in spite of the gathering dusk, as they crossed an open glade, going toward the river on the west side of the bend. One pitched from his horse. Panic-stricken, the others fled.

"Crowd 'em, fellers!" yelled Randy. "Get 'em as they cross the river at the old ford."

On through the timber they tore, running into thickets of mustang grape and bamboo, halting to get the sound of hoofs, then on again. Finally, they came out on the river bank, just as five horsemen rode out on the bar on the other side.

Two carbines cracked. One was Dolly's and the other was in the hands of Shorty, whose big mouth spread in a wide grin. He had jerked the gun from Sank's saddle. They saw one man fall, and another grip his saddle horn and lean over, as he plunged into the brush on the other side. Dolly had got a man, so that made three down and one crippled, out of six—and not one of the Railroad men had a scratch, except from briers.

"What the hell did you grab my carbine for?" growled Sank, as silence followed the fusillade of shots.

"Why, Cub and me didn't have any guns."

"No guns! What did you come along for?"

"Just company, I reckon," grinned Shorty. "Anyway, I got one and crippled another so the dogs can ketch him."

Shorty was the most uncompromising fighter in the Railroad outfit. He always grinned, whichever way the fight was going. He had grinned when Bell Holderness and Lav Tarleton took his gun—grinned because he knew they were making a mistake by not killing him. He meant to kill Bell Holderness and grin at him as he died.

"Well, we'd better stay on this side," said Randy. "The woods are likely to be full of 'em on the other side of the river."

"Apt to be plenty more on this side," said Sankey. "We better—"

"There goes one! Gimme back that gun!" yelled Shorty, as a horseman sprang out of a thicket and headed back up the river trail toward the narrows.

"Don't shoot!" called Randy. "Let's take him alive and make him talk. Come on, Dolly."

Up the trail they thundered in pursuit. It was half a mile to the spot where Randy's horse had been shot from under him earlier in the day. It was a dangerous spot, but they paid no attention to that.

The fleeing horseman didn't have a chance. He was poorly mounted and a poor rider. He didn't try to shoot, but seemed to have his whole soul centered on going away from where he was to somewhere else. As they caught up to him, Randy went on one side and Dolly on the other. Randy reached out, caught the back of his collar, and fairly lifted him from his saddle.

"Oh, Lawd, he done got me now!" moaned the prisoner, as Randy dropped him on the ground and dismounted.

"Pompey, what the devil are you doing in here, this time of day?" demanded Randy. "Don't you know this bend is full of killers?"

"Y-y-y-yassir, yassir, I know it now, Mistuh Randy, but—oh, Lawd, help me! Please, Mistuh Randy, don't you 'member that night I help you on yo' horse out at the mouth of the avenoo, when you—when yo' horse wouldn't stand still? Oh, Lawdy, save me now!"

"Shut up, fool!" snapped Randy, shaking the frightened negro boy as if he were a bundle of rags, which in fact he was. "Catch his pony, Dolly, and let's get away from this place."

They put Pompey on his pony, and all rode back into the bend. Out in the round-up prairie, where no one could slip up on them, they stopped. It was growing dark, but Pompey's eyes and teeth showed white in his shiny black face. That face was mostly eyes and teeth anyway.

He was a skinny little fellow, and perhaps the most skillful and adroit liar on the Tarleton plantation, but he never lied when he was scared, and he was frightened within one inch of his life now. He had been caught fairly in the middle of the battle, as it swept on toward the river, and had run into a thicket like a rabbit. Then, as things quieted down, he had tried to run out of trouble, and here he was.

"Which way did you come in here?" asked Randy.

"I—I come down the river trail, Mistuh Randy."

"Didn't you know it was dangerous on that trail?"

"Nossir, I didn't, but I does now. Oh, Lawdy! Miss Zella, she didn't say nothin' about dat to me. O-o-o, Lawd, save a poor nigger—"

"Shut up! What did Miss Zella have to do with it?"

"Why—she have everything they is to do with it," returned Pompey, quieting down a bit, but still shaking with fright. "She sont me—sont me—to—to bring this here to you," and suddenly remembering his errand, he pulled a note from somewhere among his rags and handed it to Randy.

"Hum! It's too dark to see to read it, and we can't make a light here. Too good a target. Keep him here until I get back, boys. If he tries to get away, shoot his liver out," and smiling at Pompey's fright, Randy mounted, and rode on toward the ranch house alone.

* * * *

As he galloped that half mile, with the note in his hand, Randy thought of many things. Life seemed dark and forbidding before him, but one ray of light shone out of the darkness. Zella was still

41

true to him. She still cared enough for him to send him a note, dangerous as it was to send it, and despite the trouble it might make for her if her father and brothers learned by any chance that she was communicating with him.

He wondered now why he hadn't been man enough to cut out his wild behavior and claim Zella as his own, long ago. That couldn't be helped now, but she should never have cause to think he was wild and irresponsible again. When this mess was over—

He dismounted and hurried to his room, the big room that had been occupied together by the three brothers, from their childhood. The grim, silent, thoughtful Asa, of whom he had always been a little afraid, was not in his familiar seat in the chimney corner. The gentle, kindly Peyton was not by the table with his book.

There was no light in the room. Randy struck a match and lit the lamp on the table. Pate's book still lay there. He glanced at the mantel and saw Asa's pipe and tobacco box. Loneliness gripped him like an icy hand. He tore open the note, and with changing countenance, read:

Dear Randy:

I'm writing this because I feel that your death and the death of your father could not bring back my dead brother and heal the wound of my father. My brothers and the Holderness brothers have sworn to kill you and your father.

I don't want to see you killed. There are many other places in the world where you could live out your life. Go while you can and hide yourself from the certain death that awaits you here. There have been many sad moments in the years that I have loved you, but the saddest is now, when I say—good-by.

I call you that from long habit. I can't remember when I didn't call you that, but now, all is done. I am writing this saddest note of my life, for the sake of that past. I tried hard to believe you were not guilty of the thing my brothers charged you with. There was doubt about you having

42

anything to do with Ben's death, and I clung to that doubt, oh, how I clung to it!

But when my father came home, shot in the back and dangerously hurt, from ambush; when he told me he saw you and knew that you and some of your men followed him and shot him, there could be no longer any doubt. My love for you has caused me much sorrow. I have often told you that some day you would commit a crime in one of your wild escapades, but I never thought it would be such a direct stab at my heart as this has been.

Zella.

Randy sprang to his feet, and crushed the note in his hand. That ray of light that he thought he saw was further gloom. He paced the old oak floor in rage.

"The death of me and my father won't bring back her brother, and heal her father's wound," he grated. "No, and what about my two brothers and three loyal, trusted men who were willing to fight my battles? What will bring them back? Go while the going is good, will I? If she thinks I could shoot an innocent man in the back, she never knew me. If she thinks I'm yellow enough to run away from this fight, she knows me still less!"

He sat down to the table and wrote:

Miss Tarleton:

I have your note, and thank you for any good intentions it may have contained, but they are wasted. I have never shot a man in the back, and never shall, unless he commits an assault on me, and then runs, as has happened more than once since this trouble. I can't understand the purpose of your note. If it was to get information as to my purpose, you shall have it. Silver Bend and the Railroad Ranch is my home, and I mean to stay here.

Until now, I have shrunk from the thought of a clash with your brothers. Now, since you tell me that they have allied themselves with my enemies, I shall welcome the day when we meet. You say my death will not bring back your brother. You didn't mention anything that would bring back my two brothers. They were both murdered, if not by your brothers, at least by their allies, and, I take it, with their sanction. I mean that some one shall atone for the death of my brothers. If anything in this note will bring comfort to my enemies, they are welcome so to construe it.

Randolph Ross.

Randy folded the note, put it in an envelope, and placed it in his pocket. He struck a match, set fire to Zella's note, and dropped it in the back of the old fireplace. He watched it burn. Thus ended his hope of happiness with the only woman he'd ever love.

* * * *

He stole out, mounted his horse, and rode back to where he had left his men with Pompey. He didn't want his father to know about these notes; this was his personal affair. When he got back to the men, he said:

"Boys, I don't want it known that I got that note. Go on to the house and eat. Take the mail in, Shorty, but don't say anything about what happened up at town to-day, unless dad questions you. There may be a lot more to tell when I get back, and—"

"When you get back! Where are you going?" asked Dolly.

"Just now, I'm going to take Pompey up to the top of the hill and send him home by the prairie road. He'd get killed before he got halfway through the narrows. You boys go on and eat. Anything I'd eat would poison me the way I feel now."

"I'm not hungry, either," declared Dolly. "I'll go with you. One lone man ain't got much business prowling the bend right now."

Randy said nothing, but he felt much. This little blue-eyed puncher was beginning to mean a great deal to him. Pompey got on his pony and was given the note. Escorted by Randy and Dolly, he took the trail that led out to the prairie. Out on the prairie they stopped.

"Here, Pompey," said Randy, and gave the boy a silver dollar.

"Thanky, suh, Mist' Randy. You're the onliest one that ever did give me a whole, borned dollar at one time, 'ceptin' Mist' Ben, and he won't never give me no more."

44

"No, and that's likely to be the last one I'll ever give you. Now, listen to me. Keep your eyes open. If you see anybody on the prairie, don't let 'em come to you. When you hit the bottom, ride that pony."

"Yas, suh, boss! When I hits dat dark ole bottom, I'm gwine make this old pestletail bronc think the ha'nts is ridin' him!"

"Well, go on."

"But, er, Mist' Randy—"

"What is it?"

"If you ever needs me, you knows whar I is. You 'bout the onliest white man I got left since Mist' Ben is gone."

"All right. If I ever need you I'll call for you. If you deliver that note to anybody but Miss Zella, I'm likely to call for you pretty soon and bring a rope."

"Oh, Lawdy, Mist' Randy! Don't talk that way, and me got to go thoo that ole dark bottom. I ain't heavy enough to break my own neck, if you did hang me. Come on here, pony, we's got to travel."

Pompey rode away into the night. Randy and the little puncher sat silently listening until the hoof beats died out.

Randy made no move to turn back toward the ranch. Dolly sat his horse in silence. Great stories are told of ancient knights and their loyal squires. Never was there a greater knight than Randy Ross was at that moment, nor was there ever a more loyal squire than Dolly.

He had been watching Randy all the year he had been at the Railroad. He had envied that stalwart height, the broad shoulders, and perfect form. He had envied Randy's education. Perhaps he had envied most of all the ease with which Randy could jerk his gun on a running horse and kill a leaping jack rabbit.

He had envied him all this, watching the devil-may-care Randy in the days before he got "busted," as Dolly called it. Since that night, when Randy had reacted so wonderfully to the acid test, and had come out of it so much a man, Dolly's envy had turned to a sort of worship. He was ready to follow Randy anywhere, no matter how wild the adventure, or how slim the chances of coming out of it alive.

* * * *

"Dolly," said Randy at last, "I don't suppose my private affairs would interest you. Maybe you didn't even know that I had expected to marry Zella Tarleton."

"Sankey told me something about it that evening we found you at the Cottonwood saloon. We saw her, and—It was sorty for her that I talked to you like I did."

"Then I have to thank her for a service, if she caused you to make a man of the sorry thing I was then."

"I didn't make a man of you," disclaimed Dolly. "I knew you was a thoroughbred all the time. I—I just sorty rode you and quieted you some, and then you done the rest yourself."

"All right, I'll thank you for the riding, but let that all go. I won't forget it. What I'm going to tell you is that everything between Zella and me is over. She told me in that note that she believed I shot her father in the back. When a woman can believe a thing like that of a man, it's time for things to be over. I'm just telling you that, so you'll understand something else I'm going to tell you."

"But maybe she ain't had a square deal, Randy. Maybe somebody has stacked the deck on her. She don't look to me like a girl that would deal from the bottom of the deck on a fellow."

"Oh, yes, she does understand. She advised me to run. To get out of this mess while the going was good. To play the part of the yellow pup that I used to be."

"No!"

"Yes. But, Dolly, I won't do it. If she had thrown me cold a week ago I might have gone to the devil. I may go anyhow, but not the way I would have gone then. She was all there was in the world to keep me half straight then. There's something else to keep me straight now."

Randy stopped, raised a gauntleted hand to the starry heaven, and went on: "If God lets me live, I'll avenge my two brothers and the loyal men who fell fighting for the Railroad, regardless of whom

46

it may hurt. I held back from tangling with the Tarleton boys. I kept my temper when the old judge talked to dad like he was a dog; all on account of Zella. She has freed me from any obligations. From here on the Tarletons and Holdernesses look alike to me. Let's go."

They turned back down the steep trail that led into Silver Bend and the Railroad ranch. Dolly said nothing, but he was puzzled. Well, he knew Randy hadn't shot the old judge, and was pretty sure he didn't kill Ben. Randy was getting a dirty deal, and he was for him, no matter what he might do from here on.

CHAPTER VI

Randy Seeks Information

They had reached the bottom before either of them spoke again. Randy stopped and Dolly came up to him.

"Dolly, I've got to find out something. I don't know anything about the H Bar ranch. Never was there in my life. Dad has peculiar ideas. He never would let his cattle drift across onto the Indian lands, even when grass was short on this side and going to waste over there. He always said he never had taken anything that didn't belong to him, and that grass didn't belong to him."

"Well, I reckon he was right about it."

"Yes, I'm sure he was. He said it would keep him out of trouble with fellows on that side, but it hasn't done it. I don't want any of their grass, but I do want to know something about what I'm fighting. I've got to have some information."

"Huh! How are you goin' to get it?"

"Go after it."

"Go to the H Bar, you mean?"

"Yes, if necessary."

"Why, Randy, that Holderness gang would shoot us so full of holes we'd make a picket fence look like a solid wall."

"Maybe not. We've got to get our hands on one of that gang and make him talk."

"Oh, thataway. Sure, come on; let's go."

"Wait a minute. We might find one of them in the cottonwoods, across the river, watching the narrows."

"I think you will find one there," said Dolly grimly, "if somebody ain't packed him off, and you'll find two more layin' on the sandbar on the other side of the river, but you won't get much information from them."

"No, I suppose not. You know that boat the boys built last summer. Know where it is?"

"Yes. It's at the upper end of the slough, but we can't go to the H Bar in a boat. It's four or five mile from the river, up at the edge of the prairie," Dolly pointed out.

"I know, but maybe we won't have to go to the H Bar. We may find what we want closer than that," Randy said with cold menace.

"Meaning what?"

"That somebody stays in that thicket of cottonwoods all the time. They shoot at everybody that goes from the Bend toward Willow Mills, and at nobody that comes this way. We can row up the river on this side, close in to the bank, and they'll never see us. Just above the thicket, we can drift across, tie up our boat, and take a look. I've got to investigate that thicket, and they've shown us that we can't do it in the daytime."

"They shore have. That sounds all right. Let's go," said Dolly.

"Easy, then. They're likely to be anywhere. We'll leave our horses in the big grape thicket this side of the slough."

Their horses hidden, they pushed the boat through the upper end of the slough into the river. Dolly was no seaman.

"All I can do is sit still and look scared," he said in a low tone.

"Just keep quiet and keep your eyes open. I'll work the boat." With noiseless strokes of the short oar, Randy sent the boat upstream.

In the marshes, around that thicket of cottonwoods, frogs were keeping up an incessant din that would cover any noise the boat might make. Well above the thicket they crossed to the other side, got out and tied the boat to a sapling and went ashore.

"We've got to be careful now," whispered Randy. "It's two or three hundred yards down this little point to where their sharpshooters take their stand."

They stole softly on through the dense thicket and had gone a hundred yards when Randy put his hand behind him and touched Dolly.

"Listen!" he whispered.

* * * *

49

There was the sound of two men walking. They were coming along a trail from opposite directions, and, crouching in the thicket close to the ground, Randy and his little puncher heard them meet.

"Hello, Steve! That you?"

"Yes," replied a growling voice.

"Well, sit down here on this log. I got a mouthful to tell you."

"Go ahead and tell it."

"Well, I come in here awhile ago to relieve Red. I went down to the stand, and Red was layin' there dead."

"Hell he was!"

"Yes. Some of that Railroad outfit potted him. Are you and Bell sure you can handle this mess the way you set out to do? Because, if you ain't, I aim to slide out while the sliding is good."

"Of course we're sure," Steve said angrily. "We've already got Asa and Pate. That just leaves Old Railroad to lead the fight, and he won't last long."

"What about Randy?"

"Nothing. He don't amount to anything if he's alive, and I don't reckon he is. The Tarleton boys are rearin' to get him, and Bell aimed to run 'em together to-day."

"Huh! Bell is a pretty smooth schemer, but I don't understand him starting this mess the way he did."

"Bell didn't start it. I started it, and he gave me hell for it. Bell's too cautious. We been ready to clean up on the Railroad outfit for a month, and Bell kept putting me off. We could 'a' got 'em one at a time, and nobody known it. Bell's idea was to go over there to the round-up and look things over. Then the next day we'd begin to work on 'em."

"Well, why didn't you work it that way?"

"We would, but trouble is, Bell was after one thing and I was after something else. All I wanted was to clean up the whole Ross outfit, because old Railroad killed my daddy. Began to look to me like Bell never would do anything, so when I got a good chance I let Asa have it. He was the only one I was afraid of."

"Why didn't you get all of 'em?"

"Get, nothing! The whole outfit came foggin' after us like a bat out of hell, and we run! Then as we went into the timber, Bell shot Ben Tarleton."

"What for?"

"I asked Bell that. He said it had to be done. Said in a pinch we could say Ben shot Asa. Besides that, Ben being shot that way, old Judge Tarleton and the other two boys would think the Railroad outfit done it."

"Bell's smooth, ain't he?"

"Yes, he's smooth, but he's too slow. We'd orto cleared up on Railroad and his boys, and gone on back home. Everybody knows Railroad killed pap, and nobody would blame us, but Bell wants too much."

"What is it he wants?"

"He wants Silver Bend. Says it's the best tract of land on either side of the river from head to mouth. Thinks when they ain't nobody left but the old woman he can get it at his own price, and he can. Another thing he wants is Zella Tarleton, and when Randy Ross is out of the way he'll get her. Oh, he'll get what he wants. He always does." Steve's tone showed his confidence in his brother's shrewdness.

"Why don't a gang just ride over to the Railroad, call Railroad and Randy out, and—"

"Two good reasons. One is, these messes have got to look like gun fights, in case there should be any hereafter about it. The other is that Bell and me wants to stay here awhile yet. Calling Railroad and Randy out and shooting them up wouldn't be no healthy job."

"I thought you said Randy don't amount to anything."

"He don't, Bill. He's yellow all the way through. But still and all, if he was cornered thataway—he's the fastest and best shot in this country."

"Well, what's the program?" asked the other. The listeners had identified him by now as Bill Hayden of the Holderness gang.

"Just to watch for Railroad and Randy and get 'em. Your job is to watch that trail, and you better get on it. Old Railroad ain't afraid of the devil. He'll be riding up to Willow Mills, and give you a chance. Bell will make the Tarleton boys get Randy, and then we'll be in the clear of everything."

"Maybe so. I don't like the idea of goin' down there and keepin' watch on that trail, with Red layin' there dead," Bill admitted.

"He can't hurt you. I'll send some of the boys to get him as soon as I get back to the ranch. Keep your eyes open. Remember that every Railroad puncher you get will make the rest quit that much quicker when Railroad's gone, and—

"What's that!"

* * * *

In his pent-up rage, Randy had moved and broken a twig beneath him. Steve Holderness and his hired killer sprang up from the log and stood for a moment listening. There was no chance to take the two killers in the darkness, so Randy had to lie still.

"Varmint in the bushes," said Hayden at last.

"Reckon so," replied Steve. "Get on the job, and if anybody comes along do as good shooting as you did when you got Pate Ross and that old puncher."

They parted, and their steps died away in the distance. Presently, Randy heard the thudding of a horse's hoofs, as Steve mounted and rode for the H Bar.

"What are we going to do now?" whispered Dolly.

"We're going to get Hayden," replied Randy, in a tense whisper. "He killed Pate, and I'm not going to wait for any law. We'll give 'em some of their own medicine. From here on, I fight the devil with fire."

Silently they waited for half an hour, then found the trail and walked on down toward the river, letting their footsteps be plainly heard. As they approached the river, a low voice said:

"You boys come for Red? Got here mighty quick."

"Met Steve on the trail, and he sent us on," replied Randy in a low tone.

"Well, come and get him. I'll be glad when he's gone," and Hayden turned his back to lead the way to where the body lay.

The next moment Hayden lay on the ground, knocked out by a blow on the head from Randy's gun.

"We've got to get away from here!" said Randy. "Come on, those fellows may get here any time," and, picking up the unconscious Hayden, he led the way to the boat.

When Hayden came back to the world, he was lying on the ground under a big tree that overhung the river at the narrows, and near the spot where Pate and old Leck had fallen. His hands and feet were tied, and he felt something at his neck.

"Whu—what are you fellows doing?" asked Hayden, groggily.

"Just waiting for you to wake up," said Dolly. "We're in a sorty hurry. Got anything to say before you go?"

"Go where?"

"I'd hate to say," and Dolly pulled the rope slightly.

"You fellows ain't going to hang me!"

He would have ended in a yell, but the rope jerked taut, and he rose endwise from the ground, kicked a few times, and was still. They made the rope fast and left him there. Without a word, Randy turned and led the way to their horses. Just before they mounted he said:

"Dolly, I know all I want to know now. We've got the man that killed Pate. I mean to hang Steve Holderness for killing Asa. The Tarletons can settle their own scores for the killing of Ben. I don't know any better punishment for them than for Zella to marry Bell Holderness and then find out about that."

"You're too hard, Randy," said Dolly. "She don't know all that. The Tarletons believe you killed Ben, and the old judge told her you shot him."

"Yes, I'm hard. Hard as hell itself. I've had plenty to make me hard. I'll make Silver Bend safe before I'm through, if you'll stay with me. Even if I have to hang a man to every tree in it."

"I'll stay with you, when it comes to cleaning up the Holderness gang, but I wish you wouldn't be so hard on Miss Zella. She—"

"Never mind. Don't mention her name to me again, and you and I will get along finely," and, mounting his horse, Randy led the way on to the ranch.

In a little more than forty-eight hours Randolph Ross had changed from a wild, irresponsible boy to a strong, purposeful man. And in the last few hours, since reading Zella's note and hearing Steve and Hayden talk, he had turned to a hard man, with but one purpose in life—bitter, bitter vengeance.

He wanted to kill the men who had robbed him of his brothers. He wanted to humble the woman whom he had loved with all his soul because she had doubted him when he was in trouble. He was far on the road to becoming a very bad and dangerous man, and, as the canker ate farther into his heart, he would become worse.

* * * *

Wise little Dolly knew this. He could see that what he thought he had made into a wonderful man was likely to become a hideous monster.

Randy Ross was desperate now. He would go to any length to put a rope on Steve's neck. Dolly was willing to follow him in that enterprise, but when that was done he wanted to see Randy and Zella happy. As he rode silently along with Randy, he made a resolution to save this naturally fine young man from himself.

When they reached the ranch, Dolly went on to the bunk shack. Randy would have asked him to share that big, lonesome room, for company, but there was such a storm in his soul that Ross wanted solitude, and a chance to think things out. He slipped into the house, but didn't escape the ears of old Railroad. His father was in bed, but hadn't been asleep, though it was some time after midnight. Randy made a light. He had eaten nothing since noon, but he wasn't hungry and felt that he could never sleep again.

Barely had he sat down to his task of thinking when the door opened and old Railroad entered. His hair was tousled, and he was in nightshirt and trousers, with one suspender down.

"Randy, I'm mighty glad you come in. I couldn't go to sleep. I went out and asked the boys about you. They said you and Dolly went off somewheres, but they didn't know where."

"Some of 'em knew. They were lying to you for me, like always. That's got to be stopped. I'm not going to do anything more that I'm ashamed for you to know, or that you'll be ashamed to know. I'll tell you where I went. You ought to know it."

Randy recapitulated the day's events. He told of the killing of Brazos and Keech by Bell Holderness and Lav Tarleton. He told of the running fight in the woods and of capturing Pompey. Railroad's lips twisted in a wintry smile at thought of Pompey's fright. Then Randy told of the note from Zella and what he had written to her.

"I'm mighty sorry about that, Randy. Zella is as fine a young woman as there is in the world. She just don't understand."

"Don't, dad! When you excuse her, I feel like you're accusing me. She didn't have any right to think that I'd do the things they accuse me of doing. She ought to know I couldn't do it. I hope she marries Bell, and then finds out that he shot Ben in the back."

"Stop, Randy! Don't be so bitter!"

"Why shouldn't I be bitter?"

"But you don't know that Bell shot Ben. That was just a guess of ours."

"Oh, yes, I do know it," and Randy went on to tell of the trip to the thicket and the hanging of Hayden.

"Thank God that it wasn't my bullet that killed Ben," said Railroad, fervently. "Judge Tarleton and I have been friends and neighbors always. He's hot-headed and jumps to conclusions, but he's a good man."

"Good man or not, the Tarletons have tied in with the Holdernesses, and they all look alike to me. I'm not going to hunt the Tarleton boys, but they're hunting me and they can find me."

"Randy, I'd hate—"

"Let's don't talk about that, dad. If we meet, we meet, and that's all there is to it. We found out that Hayden killed Pate, and we hanged him. We heard Steve say he shot Asa, and I'll hang him if I live."

* * * *

"That's all right for them, Randy, but it ought to stop there."

"What about Bell? He's the prime mover in the whole mess," and Randy went over the two reasons Steve had given for Bell's part in the mess.

"Bell ought to hang, too, then. He'll never get Silver Bend."

"Not while I live," Randy vowed.

"Not while anybody lives. Mother and I will make a will that, in the event of your death, we'll leave it to your uncle for his lifetime, and then to his heirs. He won't want it, but he can't sell it."

"That's going a long way around. I know a better way than that to keep Bell from getting it. I don't want to kill him now. I want him to marry Zella.

"Then, after they are married, I want to show her proof that he shot Ben in the back and had her father shot. After that, I'm ready to shoot Bell, or hang him, whichever comes handiest."

Railroad was appalled at his son's bitterness. Deep in his heart, he wanted Randy to marry Zella, had always wanted it. That very day he had thought of it much. The farmer and his plow were encroaching on the cow country. A few more years and that would be a farming country.

A little work—and Railroad had plenty of money to have it done—and Silver Bend would be a great plantation, five or six times larger than the Tarleton plantation, and better, because the alluvial soil was new and fresh. Randy was the only heir now. It would all be his. With a wife like Zella, a woman of fine breeding and culture, and plenty of money, Randy could go a long way in life. But Randy had dashed all those hopes. Railroad sat with bowed head as Randy went on:

"We can't take the men and go into this fight, as you did in old times, and shoot it out in the open. They won't come out in the open. If we went to the H Bar we might find half a dozen men, and maybe none. They're going to bushwhack and get Railroad riders when and where they can. More than two men together will simply make a better target for them. I'm going to take Dolly in the morning, and hunt where I think the hunting is good. The other men had better work the cattle out onto the prairie and keep them there until this is over, one way or another."

"Maybe you're right," said Railroad, wearily, "but don't take too many chances, son. You're all I got left now. I wish I could ride with you, but I can't. I'm still good for a minute, but I don't last out. My heart beats too fast. I reckon I driv it too much when I was younger. Go to bed and get some sleep. When we get up in the morning, things never look to us like they did the day before," and Railroad tottered off to bed, his mind also full of plans for saving this last son from a life of misery and bitterness.

CHAPTER VII

Who Killed Asa Ross?

Lights burned late in two rooms of the Tarleton house that night. One of these was the great bedroom on the ground floor, where the judge lay, painfully, but not seriously wounded. The bullet had passed through the top of the left hip, grazing it, but not breaking it. The doctor had said it would get well, with proper care, and the patient was now sleeping under the influence of an opiate.

The other light was in Zella's room. A little while after nightfall she had slipped out to the cabin back of the house, where the family servants lived. She asked for Pompey, and was told that he had not come in. On her way to the house she was upbraiding herself for having sent the faithful negro into trouble, when a low voice called her:

"Miss Zella! Miss Zella, here I is," and Pompey stole toward her in the darkness.

"What kept you so long?" she asked.

"Miss Zella, I been skeered outen my nacherl bawn witses," and Pompey proceeded to tell a highly colored story of his adventures in a hurried whisper.

"Did you give Mr. Randy the note?"

"Yes'm, I sholy did, and he gimme a note for you, an'—now where at is that old note," and Pompey fumbled among his rags. "Here she is, an' I's glad to get rid of her. Mist' Randy, say if I give it to anybody else he gwine hang me good."

"All right, Pompey. Run along now. I'll give you something in the morning."

Zella put the note in the front of her dress and went back into the house.

"Huh! Look lak I gwine to come out of this alive yit. Gwine gimme something in the mawnin'. Hope it ain't no more job like that'n. That ol' dark bottom, hoo-oo!" and he went on to the cabin

58

where supper and an expert job of lying about where he had been, were in prospect.

Zella stole up the stair to her room, entered, and locked the door. No one in that house, except herself and the faithful Pompey, would ever know of this note. A hundred times she had received notes in the same manner from Randy, when he had been on one of his escapades. They had always been so penitent and so full of love that she could but yield and give him a chance to make amends.

But this time she couldn't yield. Almost by rote she knew what was in that note, she thought. In spite of her protestations to herself and her written message to Randy, that her love for him was a thing of the dead past, she knew in her heart, as she pressed the note to her bosom, that it was not and never could be.

She opened the note, and, with staring eyes, read the salutation, "Miss Tarleton." Tears sprang to her eyes. She brushed them away and read on to the end, then read it again. She looked about the room, as if for some one to question, then fell across the bed and wept bitterly.

After all her effort, Randy would not save himself. Never had he failed to do anything she asked him to do, when he was in a penitent mood. But he was not even penitent now. What was wrong? Randy, guilty, never would have written that. It was not the old Randy. Had he been falsely accused? At that thought, she sobbed afresh.

For an hour that day, just after noon, she had listened to Bell Holderness and her brothers discuss the killing of Ben and the shooting of her father, as they sat in the room with the judge. She had gone from that room and had written and dispatched her note to Randy, convinced, she thought, of his guilt.

Now she ceased her sobbing, and lay staring at the ceiling, trying to reason the thing out, not knowing that it is impossible to reason with love; that love is a finished, selfish quality that bears on all things, but suffers none to interfere with it. Strangest of all, delicate plant though it may be, it thrives on adversity.

As she lay puzzling over her problem, she recalled the story Bell had told of the trouble at the Railroad round-up. It had sounded all right then, but going over it now, in her mind, it didn't ring true. Bell never had said definitely who killed Asa Ross. That tormenting question sprang into her mind. "Who killed Asa Ross?" It would not down. Far toward morning, she fell asleep, with that question still revolving in her thoughts.

* * * *

Her first thought on waking was that she wanted to see Randy, had to see him. This, she knew was impossible. There was danger everywhere in Silver Bend. Then her mind veered to Bell Holderness. She wanted to see him and talk to him. She knew he had spent the night in the house. In Ben's room, in fact. She dressed hurriedly and went down to the yard.

It was a fine, balmy spring morning, and a few roses were in bloom. Zella knew a good many things. Bell Holderness was a handsome fellow, blond, with deep blue eyes, and a pleasing appearance. Bell had said nice things to her many a time. In view of the grief in the home, he had said nothing of that sort to her the day before, but his eyes had been sufficiently eloquent. She knew her attraction for him, and purposely lingered among the roses.

"Wonderful morning, Miss Zella," he said as he came up.

"Yes. It is such a pity one can't be happy on a morning like this. I've been wishing you'd come out here."

"I'd be a strange man if that didn't make me happy."

"I want to ask you something."

"I've wanted to ask you something a long, long time, but never had the courage. Ask your question first, and I'll answer it if I can."

"Who killed Asa Ross?" she shot the question like a bolt, and Bell fairly staggered.

"Why, I—I can't tell you."

"You can't tell me! You saw it, did you not?"

"Yes, but—Sometimes it is best not to know too much about such things."

Zella stood looking at him in silence. He averted his eyes and tried to talk of something else, but failed. The breakfast bell rang, and they went in. Not another word passed between them.

Soon after breakfast, Bell saddled his horse and rode to town. He was thinking of Zella more intently than he had in some time, but the thoughts were not pleasant ones. He knew she had trapped him, caught him off his guard with her question, and that he had come out of it badly. But Bell was the kind of man who can plan and wait.

Another day ought to see Randy Ross and old Railroad disposed of. Randy couldn't stay away from drink much longer. Bell didn't mean to kill Randy—nothing so coarse as that. Either of the Tarleton boys would kill Randy on sight; they had promised to follow him on to town in a little while and lay in wait for Randy. Lav and Cliff had only one purpose in mind now, and that was to meet Randy Ross and shoot it out with him.

Bell was barely out of sight when Zella sought her father. The judge was awake and feeling fairly well. Lav and Cliff were in the room when she entered.

"Do it fair and open like men," Judge Tarleton was saying. "I meant to do it myself the first time I caught either of them away from home. I don't want a boy of mine ever to turn his back to an enemy, and I'd be disgraced if I knew one of you took an unfair advantage."

"What are you talking about?" asked Zella.

"Talking about shooting Randy Ross," said Judge Tarleton calmly. "Of course, he's got to be shot after what has happened. I might let him go for shooting me from the brush, since I guess it won't kill me, but we can't overlook the killing of Ben."

"Let me ask you all a question. I asked Bell Holderness, but he wouldn't answer it."

"What is the question?" said Lav, impatiently.

"Who killed Asa Ross?"

"Why, I hadn't thought of that. He was killed in a gun fight at the Railroad round-up."

"Yes, I know, but who killed him?"

"What do you mean? Trying to leave the impression that Ben killed him?"

* * * *

"No," said Zella, slowly, "but I'm pretty sure that if anybody ever presses Bell Holderness for an answer to that question, he'll leave that impression."

"Now, Zella, you stay out of this," Lav insisted. "It's a man's job, and we'll attend to it. We are not interested in who killed Asa Ross. We know who killed Ben and we know who shot father, and that's all that concerns us."

"Yes, but are you sure you know who killed Ben, and are you sure it makes no difference who killed Asa?" persisted Zella.

"Now, Zella," ordered Lav, "I've told you to keep out of this. We'll attend to it."

But Zella had done the thing she meant to do, namely, to plant a doubt in the minds of her father and brothers. When she was gone, they sat in silence for moments.

"Now what do you suppose Zella knows?" asked the old judge at last.

"Nothing!" snapped Lav, who started when his father spoke, because he had unpleasant thoughts. He had fired one shot in the mess the day before when two Railroad punchers had been killed. He was sure he had not hit either of them, but in a way he had been a party to the killing, and it wasn't a pleasant thought.

"She's just like any other woman that goes crazy over a worthless man. She's got the habit of making excuses for Randy Ross, and she can't break herself of it."

"Why, she didn't mention Randy," said Cliff.

"I wish I knew who did kill Asa Ross," the old judge interrupted. "It might make considerable difference. Maybe you boys better stay out of this until we know more. I don't mean hide, but not hunt for him. He won't run away. He's too much like old Railroad. As Zella says, we don't know these things. We been pretty hot in the collar about Ben being killed, and about me being shot up. I didn't

62

see who shot me. All I know is that Randy and some more fellows were behind me when I entered the timber. I never did see anybody when the shot was fired."

"Well, I'm going on to town," declared Lav. "I don't mean to hole up. I can't promise what'll happen if I meet Randy."

"I'll stay here with father," said Cliff. "I think he's right. We've always found the Ross outfit on the square. If I'd met Randy yesterday I'd have opened on him, but now I don't know. Since Zella asked those questions, things look different."

But Zella had asked her questions too late, as far as Randy was concerned. The Tarleton boys had sent him word by Cub and Shorty, or at least Lav had, that they meant to kill him on sight, and Zella had written him to leave the country while he could.

He had said the Tarletons and Holdernesses all looked alike to him, and he meant it. He knew a square deal when he saw it, and he hadn't been given one.

Bell Holderness had ridden on to Willow Mills. The place was quiet as a churchyard. The men who had been killed the day before had been buried at nightfall. Willow Mills was but a mile from Red River. Such fights were common, and the town had its Boot Hill, where men who died in their boots were buried and forgotten.

* * * *

Bell went to the Cottonwood Saloon. It was not generally known, but he owned the place, and the men who worked there were his spies.

"Seen anything of Randy Ross, or any of the rest of the Railroad outfit since I was here?" he asked the bartender.

"No, sir. Had less business last night than we had for a long time. When nobody comes in from the Railroad or the H Bar, business is always dull."

"Hang business," snapped Bell. "I'm interested in locating Randy Ross just now. Where do you suppose he's getting his whisky if he don't come to town or send a hand?"

"Search me."

"I don't want to search you, but I want you fellows to get your grapevine telegraph to work and locate Randy Ross."

"That's it tickin' now, I reckon," drawled the bartender as a lone horseman came storming in from the north, and skidded to a stop in front of the Cottonwood.

It was Steve Holderness. He nodded to the barkeep, poured a drink, and gulped it. Then he nodded toward the door and went out, with Bell following him.

"What the hell are you doing on this side?" snapped Bell, when they were out in the open. "Didn't I tell you to stay on the other side and ramrod things over there? I'll handle this side."

"Yes, you did, but you didn't tie me over there. You're so strong for schemes and plans. I come over here to tell you that yore damn plans have busted, and if you don't get from under they'll fall on you."

"What do you mean?"

"I mean for one thing that Railroad Ross ain't as near dead old as you think he is. You can recollect, as well as I can, when old Railroad Ross used to be head of the Vigilantes. He hung everybody he caught with an unidentified horse, and a few more on suspicion, just for associating with horse rustlers."

"Yes, I recollect it. What of it?"

"Plenty. He ain't forgot how to handle a rope, and my neck hurts."

"Damn it, quit beating about the bush, and tell what's on your mind."

"Well, last night Hayden went down to the thicket to relieve Red and found him dead. Somebody had shot him. I went there awhile after dark, and Hayden told me about it, so I sent a couple of men to get Red. They got him all right, but Hayden was gone. Meantime Sam come in to the ranch with one leg shot half off. Him and five more of our fellows flushed a covey of Railroad punchers over in Silver Bend just at sunset, and they wouldn't fly. They got one of Sam's men on that side and two more as they crossed the river just below the thicket. Sam's shot right smart and the doc's gone out there."

"Well, what's that got to do with old Railroad and his tight-rope performance?"

"Nothing, maybe. This morning I taken some of the boys and went down to get the two dead ones and look for Hayden."

"Did you find Hayden? Tell it!"

"Yes, we found him," and Steve looked over his shoulder as if he feared the devil were behind him.

"Where?"

"Hanging in that big oak tree at the narrows, swinging round and round, round and round, in the wind, as the rope turned and twisted. Gosh, it was awful!"

"Did you go over and get him?"

"I did not, and I ain't goin' to. I taken a chance coming over here to tell you about it. That's all the business I got on this side. I'm goin' back, and stay back. If you want Hayden, you can have him."

"Yeah!" sneered Bell. "You was in such a hell of a hurry to start this mess before I was ready. Now it's beginning to pinch, your nerve is slipping, and you want to leave me the bag to hold. Go on back and hide if you want to. Randy and old Railroad won't bother anybody much longer. Some real men are going after them."

* * * *

Steve mounted his horse and rode out of town. Bell stood rolling a cigar in his mouth, and watching his brother. Bell Holderness was as cool-headed a villain as that border ever knew. He made his plans and worked to them. If something went awry, he never lost his head.

He had sat in on this game to win Silver Bend and Zella Tarleton; the stakes were high. Steve had gummed the game when he killed Asa Ross ahead of schedule, and Bell had saved the day by killing Ben Tarleton, who was supposed to belong to his gang. Now it appeared that Sam had gummed it again by going into Silver Bend against orders.

Bell had told them to stay out after Asa and Pate were killed, and he'd get Railroad and Randy. He meant to make the Tarleton boys do that job and leave him with clean hands; he still meant to do that. He turned and looked up the long lane. A lone horseman was coming toward him. The morning sun was in Bell's eyes, and he couldn't see who it was. He slipped into the saloon, spoke a few words to the bartender, and went on into a back room.

Waiting there in that little room, Bell Holderness looked like an arch fiend. His handsome face, which was a cold mask in the company of other men, gave way to a snarling distortion of rage. Another of his plans had gone wrong. The Tarleton brothers said they would follow him on to town. They hadn't done it. Now, he felt sure, Randy Ross was riding into town. He had to be killed. The Tarleton boys ought to kill him, would kill him if they met, but Randy had to be disposed of, and that quickly. He heard a step in the saloon, and a few low-spoken words at the bar. Drawing his gun, he turned the cylinder lightly, raised and lowered the hammer, and pushed the gun back loosely in the holster for a quick draw. It had come to a showdown. If the Tarleton boys didn't come pretty soon he'd go out there and have it over. He knew how Randy drank. He would pour it down greedily until he was drunk, and then—

Bell stood in the little room listening. Only a few low words were spoken, and he could catch none of them. At last he pulled himself together and pushed the door open softly. Not Randy, but Lav Tarleton, sat smoking.

"I've been waiting for you," said Lav.

"I didn't know you had come. Where's Cliff?"

"He decided not to come."

"Do you mean to take Randy Ross on by yourself?" Bell inquired.

"Yes, if I meet him, but—"

"But what?"

"Who killed Asa Ross?"

Again that question smote Bell in the face. This time it turned his face to flaming rage, but before Lav could read it, it changed to the cold, smooth, lying mask.

"Why, I—I don't know who killed him. He was killed in a gun fight."

"Were Pate Ross and old Leck killed in a gun fight, too?"

"Certainly. What difference does it make to you how those fellows were killed? They're dead and it's luck for us that they are. You know who killed your brother Ben. It was the Ross outfit. Two of them are still living, and you and Cliff would be strange brothers if you didn't get them as quick as you can, before they bushwhack you, like they did your father."

"We thought that yesterday. We've changed our minds. We're not going to hunt them. If we meet Randy or his father, we'll let things take their course."

Bell went white with the stress of his situation. Nothing but quick action could save Silver Bend and Zella for him. True to his nature, he became cooler than ever in the face of disaster. All was not lost yet. He had other tricks in his bag. Lighting a cigar, he invited Lav to take a drink.

CHAPTER VIII

Dangling Scarecrows

The Railroad ranch stirred early that morning, despite the fact that neither Randy nor his father had slept much. Things may or may not have looked different to Railroad. To Randy there had been no change, for he had not slept enough to make a curtain between the two days.

He had some plans himself and he was going to work on them. Bell Holderness and Lav Tarleton had got two of his men the day before. On the other hand, he and his men with him had scored a few times themselves. Dolly had got the man Red, in the thicket. Then they had got three more and crippled one in the running fight at sunset. Then crowning the day's work, he and Dolly had hanged Bill Hayden. Five in all.

Decidedly, they had won a trick in the game of war. The chief winning had been gaining positive knowledge of what the mess was all about. He was going to hang Steve Holderness if he could lay hands on him, for the murder of Asa, but he was bitterer against Bell than Steve. It might be that Steve had thought he was avenging his father, but with Bell, who was engineering the war, it was just a matter of greed, avarice and lust.

Randy quivered at the thought. Like all jealous people, he wanted to hurt both the persons who caused his jealousy. He wanted to kill Bell Holderness, meant to kill him. He also wanted to humiliate Zella. Not that she could ever be anything to him again, he thought, but he wanted her to suffer for her lack of faith in him.

At that moment he thought he no longer loved Zella, and wondered that he had ever loved her. It was in this bitter frame of mind that he gave the other men orders to work the cattle on the prairie, riding in pairs, and keeping a close watch. Then turning to Dolly, he said:

"Better get plenty of bread and meat in our saddle pockets. I don't know when we'll be back."

Dolly had obeyed, thoughtfully. No song had passed the lips of the usually happy little puncher since Sankey had stopped him that first day. He, too, had slept little. Randy's bitterness against Zella had set him thinking. He felt sure that if Zella knew Randy was innocent, she would fly to his arms. She might easily be convinced of Randy's innocence, but Randy had gone wild. Would he ever forgive the girl? With such thoughts in his mind, Dolly mounted and rode away with Randy.

Railroad Ross was old, but he was far from dead. He had one boy left. He felt that there might be one more little burst of speed in him. Since burying his two sons, he had sat around the house, unwilling to leave his good wife alone with her grief. His old heart had been driven too hard and was in bad shape, but his head was still all right and he had spent the night in thought. It was not enough to save Randy's life, if he could not save the boy from the bitterness that gripped his soul.

He watched Randy and Dolly ride away toward where they had left Bill Hayden hanging in the tree. A man had to be pretty bitter to want to go back and look at a thing like that. The men were mounting, when Railroad called old Con Bates and Sankey aside, and let the others go on.

"Con," he said, "you and Sankey have been with me a long time. The old Railroad is about on the rocks. You've been in messes with me before, but never one like this. The Holderness boys have picked up a new breed of killers that has drifted into that Indian country from the four corners of the earth. They don't fight like cow-people, but we got to fight 'em. I just got one boy left. If he comes out of this alive, he'll be ruined, unless—"

Railroad stopped. He never liked to tell his men too much. Presently, he went on.

"I've been in this bend more than thirty years. I've never trespassed on the other side of the river, but I may have to do it now.

You saw the two fellows that were with the Holderness boys when they killed Asa, Con?"

"Yes, sir," growled Con.

"One of 'em was a hatchet-faced, rat-mouthed, gimlet-eyed fellow they called Bud, and the other was a handsome, gray-eyed devil they called Turk. Would you know 'em if you saw 'em?"

"Yes, sir."

"Well, I want them two fellows and I want 'em alive and well. If they can be got, you two can get 'em. It may take an hour, or it may take a month. Get 'em and bring 'em here as quick as you can."

* * * *

The two wrinkled old riders mounted and rode away, not saying what they meant to do. Railroad had not definitely ordered them to go into the Indian country; but they understood him.

Railroad watched them ride north, toward the bottom of the Silver Bend bottle. He knew they were going into danger, but danger meant little to such men. If it were not for leaving his wife alone, he'd mount and ride with them. His heart might play out on him, but it would be in a good cause.

Knowing Railroad's long-standing policy of keeping to his own side of Red River, Bell had felt that his gang were safe as long as they stayed on their own side. Some one had got Hayden and hanged him, but Hayden must have disobeyed orders and suffered for it the same as Sam had.

Bell sat in the cottonwood, gnawing at his mustache, and trying to evolve a new plan, concoct a new lie, that would drive the Tarleton boys on to hunt Randy and kill him. If he had guessed just how much Randy Ross knew, and just how different he was from the old Randy, Bell would not have been so cool. Unmindful of everything, he went on, planning his next move in this perilous game.

Randy and Dolly rode west from the Railroad and entered the timber. They had seen no one, when they reached the river at the ford where the battle had taken place the evening before. This ford was just below the cottonwood thicket where so much mischief had been done. Directly across from the lower end of the thicket, Bill Hayden still swung in the wind, in plain view from the other side of the river. As they sat their horses behind a screen of brush, Dolly said:

"Shore quiet in the Bend this morning. Ain't heard a sound. Seems like hangin' that gent up has worked like it does on crows. My daddy used to kill crows and hang 'em up around his melon patch. A crow wouldn't come in a mile of it, as long as they hung there."

"Easy on the talking!" warned Randy. "Yonder they come."

Three men rode down to the ford on the opposite side of the river. Two of them were leading pack-horses. The other rider was Steve Holderness. Steve sat on his horse, while the other two men picked the bodies up from the ground and lashed them to the pack saddles. They had finished the job and were ready to go, when one of them glanced up and across the river.

"Good God! Look yonder!" he cried. "It's Bill Hayden, hanging by the neck!"

On the Railroad side of the river, Dolly fingered his gun. "I can get Steve now," he said.

"No!" Randy growled. "Let him alone. I don't want him shot. I'm going to hang him."

Steve Holderness caught an eyeful of the tight-rope performance, and hastily wheeled his horse into the brush, calling to the others to come on. Randy and Dolly sat watching until they all disappeared into the dense bottom.

"They won't be so thick around this neighborhood now," said Randy, grimly. "Come on. Let's go across and see what we can find."

Crossing the river, they followed the trail of the five horses over the soft, bottom soil. Twice they glimpsed the Holderness men through the trees, and stopped behind convenient trunks until the others went on. Climbing out of the bottom onto a stretch of open woods they came to the road that led from Willow Mills to the H Bar. Here the two H Bar men turned north with their gruesome

71

pack-horses, and Steve galloped south toward town. It was then that Steve carried the news to Bell.

"We've let 'em get plumb away!" said Dolly, in a tone of disappointment.

"No, we haven't. It's Steve that we are after. He's gone somewhere to tell the news. He'll be back."

* * * *

They turned across to where the road dipped into the bottom again, rode into a dense thicket and stopped.

"Here's where we do some bushwhacking on our own account," muttered Randy. "Damn that Holderness and Tarleton gang. I'll teach them some tricks at their own game."

Dolly shuddered at the venom in Randy's tone. It had reached the point that the little cowboy shuddered every time Randy mentioned the name of Tarleton.

An hour passed in silent listening, after that. Then they heard the thud of galloping hoofs, coming along the road from the Willow Mills crossing on the river.

"Get set!" ordered Randy.

The horseman came storming on. He was fairly abreast of the thicket when Randy's gun crashed. The horse faltered, stopped and fell. Steve Holderness rolled clear and sprang to his feet, but he was looking into two guns.

"Get your hands up!" snapped Randy. "Take his gun, Dolly. Get a horn-string and tie his hands behind him."

"What's the idea, Randy?" whimpered Steve, as he stood bound.

For reply, Randy threw a rope over a big limb that projected across the road.

"You—you ain't goin' to hang me, Randy?"

"Why not?"

"I—I got a family, and—"

"Asa had some brothers and a father and a mother," said Randy.

"I—I didn't kill Asa. It was Bell. Let me go, and I'll tell you all about it. Bell is back of this mess. I'll tell you what he wants, and tell you what he aims to do—before he does it!"

"I know what he aims to do. Let him do it, if he can. Rope him, Dolly."

There was one wild, gurgling scream, and Steve Holderness swung above the road, in his death struggle.

"That'll do for to-day," Randy said, thoughtfully, as they crossed the river into Silver Bend. "I haven't slept much the last few nights, and I'm about all in. That'll give the Holderness and Tarleton gang something to think about, as soon as they find it out. They'll find it out, too, for somebody will be going from the H Bar to keep Bell advised about what is going on over here."

There were but two safe places that they could rest. One of these was the ranch house. Randy didn't want to go there. He wanted to be alone with his bitterness and his hate.

To be with Dolly was as near being alone as it was possible to be in human company, for he rarely spoke now unless he was spoken to.

The only other safe place was out on the prairie, where no one could ride up on them unseen. Already, Randy was becoming a wild man in some ways. He had been advised that Bell Holderness and the Tarleton boys were hunting him, and he had become watchful.

It was well after noon when they stopped at a clump of trees on a high point, far out on the prairie. They ate a little lunch, then rolled smokes. Suddenly, Dolly stretched out on the ground, and in an instant, fell asleep.

Randy looked at the little puncher in surprise. He himself was not in the least sleepy, though he had slept very little for three nights. He had heard that insane people didn't sleep, and wondered if his own mind was unbalanced. No, he told himself, he was not crazy—yet.

Randy supposed that Dolly had simply been overcome by need of sleep, and couldn't stay awake. The fact was that it was some time before Dolly really went to sleep. He had feigned sleep deliberately, for he knew Randy would have to sleep some time, and Dolly wanted to be awake, and very much awake, when that young man finally succumbed to the demands of nature.

Randy had plenty of time to think, undisturbed. He watched Dolly as he lay sleeping, as peacefully as if nothing had happened to excite his mind. This little man had done much for him. Had it not been for Dolly, he would have gone on a debauch the night his brothers were killed. Had it not been for Dolly, he would never have been man enough to face this situation.

And so his thoughts ran on, taking all the incidents for the last three days. It was far toward night when Dolly opened his baby-blue eyes, looked about him, and glanced at the sun.

"Reckon I must have slept a nap."

"About four hours," said Randy. "We'd better ride from here if we want to get home before night."

They rode back into Silver Bend, seeing no one as they went. When they came out on the little prairie, they saw four riders just approaching the ranch. Two of them they recognized as Con and Sankey. The other two, they didn't know. When they reached the ranch, old Railroad was talking to the two strangers, whom Randy recognized as the man called Bud and the one called Turk, who had been at the round-up with the Holderness boys.

"What do you want with us?" demanded Turk.

"I don't know yet," drawled old Railroad. "I don't aim to hang you for awhile. If you tell the truth, I may not hang you at all."

"That sounds fair," smiled the handsome Turk, while Bud scowled and darted a vicious look from his gimlet eyes. "What's this truth you want told about?"

"Who killed Asa, who killed Ben Tarleton, and who shot the judge?"

"Don't you know?"

"Yes, we know, but we want to see if you fellows would rather tell the truth about it than be hanged."

"Don't squeal, Turk!" snarled Bud. "They don't know nothin'."

"Maybe not," laughed Turk, "but I'd rather be a live welcher than a dead stayer. Shoot your questions, Mr. Ross, one at a time."

"All right. Who killed Asa?"

"Steve."

"Who killed Ben?"

"Bell Holderness."

"Who shot Judge Tarleton?"

"Red Mangus."

"You know all that, do you?"

"Yes, sir. I saw Steve and Bell do the killing, and I was in ten feet of Red, when he shot the judge, and got shot for his trouble. I didn't even tell anybody Red was dead. I don't believe in laying in the brush and potting people."

"Is he telling the truth, Bud?"

"Oh, hell! Yes, that's right."

"All right. There's a new log smokehouse with a door that you can't break. I'm going to put you in there, give you grub and blankets, and lock the door. When I call on you again, if you tell the same story, I may turn you loose. If you don't—"

Randy listened to all this without a word. When the men were locked in and he and his father went to the house, he asked:

"What was the idea of all that? We know we didn't shoot Judge Tarleton. What difference does it make, anyway? We'll have to shoot the judge and the boys, all three, whenever we meet them. Better hang these two, while you can."

"I give 'em my word, Randy, and my word's generally pretty good. They've got some law on this side of the river, and we're apt to need witnesses before this mess is over."

Randy didn't believe his father was likely to pay much attention to law in a mess like this, but he didn't argue the matter. Instead, he said:

"All right. We'll talk about that in the morning. I didn't know I was sleepy until right now. I want to eat something and go to bed."

Railroad didn't insist on knowing what had happened that day. In half an hour Randy was asleep in bed. He couldn't have kept awake even if he had known what would happen while he slept—and he didn't know.

CHAPTER X

Dolly Tells the Truth

Judge Tarleton lay on his bed. Cliff sat beside him, facing the door, as Dolly entered. Lav, his dark brows drawn in a scowl, stood just back of Cliff's chair. This man was a Railroad rider. Old Railroad Ross had admitted some man of his outfit had killed Ben. It was well known that the men of the Railroad outfit stuck together as one man. This little red-haired, blue-eyed manikin was one of them, for all his boyish looks.

He might be the very man who had fired the fatal shot.

Zella started to introduce him, realized that she didn't know his name, and halted.

"Never mind the introduction," said the judge. "We know he belongs to the Railroad outfit, and that's enough. What have you got to say for yourself, young man?"

Dolly saw that he was starting into this interview with a handicap. It was the handicap of being a Railroad puncher, but he kept his wits about him.

"You fellows think Randy shot the judge. I'm here to tell you that he didn't. The man who shot you, judge, was an H Bar man called Red. He's dead."

"How do you know he's dead?"

"I killed him about five minutes after he shot you."

"You killed him? You talk mighty cool about killing men."

"I am right cool about killing a man that lays in the brush and shoots innocent men like they were sheep-killing dogs."

"Huh! Well, I'm not hurt very bad. What my boys and me have against the Railroad outfit is the killing of my son Ben at the round-up."

"They didn't kill him."

"Didn't kill him! Why, Railroad Ross himself told me they did, and whatever else he is, Railroad is not a liar. We don't know a great deal about that fight that day, but we've got some friends, and they told us part of it. Enough to satisfy us that—"

"Beg pardon, sir, but did they tell you who killed Asa Ross, and what for?"

There was that question again.

"No!" thundered the judge. "We are not interested in that. If you came here to insinuate that Ben killed—"

"I didn't. I came here to get word to you that the Railroad outfit didn't kill Ben, and that Randy didn't shoot you. Instead of hunting Randy to kill him, you ought to be helping him against his enemies."

"Oh, Randy's begging for help, is he?" put in Lav.

Dolly turned his blue eyes on Lav, and for once the stalwart Tarleton, patrician though he was, quailed before a glance from a pair of baby-blue eyes.

Dolly was dangerously near an explosion, but he checked himself.

"No. Randy isn't asking for any more help than he's got. He don't need any more. He don't know I came here. I took a chance on getting killed to help you."

"Keep quiet, Lav," said the judge, as Lav opened his mouth to speak. "Now, young man, this farce has gone far enough. I gave my word to my daughter that you wouldn't be harmed if you came here. There is just one question that we want answered. Who killed Ben?"

The crisis had come. Dolly pulled himself together. He was pitted against the champion liar and coldest schemer in the world, but he came up to the scratch.

"Bell Holderness."

* * * *

"No!" cried the three men together, while Zella, standing in the door, clenched her hands until the nails cut the flesh.

"You can't get away with that!" cried Lav. "Bell has been our friend all through this trouble, and still is. You can't stand here in this house and try to blacken the name of our friend."

White-faced, Lav took a step forward, with fists clenched. Dolly stood his ground, a narrow white line showing along the edge of his lips.

"Lav!" called the old judge. "My word is out that this boy won't be mistreated in my house. And after all, he's just a hired man, doing what he is told to do."

"A minute, judge," and Dolly's voice hummed with the tenseness of it. "I told you that nobody sent me here. I am just a hired man, but my word is as good as yours. Friend or no friend, Bell Holderness killed your son."

"Would you like to face Bell Holderness with that statement?" snapped Lav.

"Yes! I'd like to face him, but not alone, when he's got a gang of killers with him, like he had when he murdered Keech and Brazos."

The shot went home. To be classed as one of the H Bar gang was too much for Lav. He went white to his lips and recoiled a step. Dolly saw what was in his eyes. Lav was insulted, and to insult a Tarleton was to seek deadly danger. Dolly knew some sort of showdown was imminent.

He had taken a positive stand. He might not get shot there in the house, but Lav would meet him as soon as he got away from the premises. A tense moment followed Dolly's statement. A Tarleton had been charged by innuendo of being a member of a gang of cold killers.

Finally Lav spoke. "I guess you know what you've done, and there is only one way out of it. I'm not asking you to do that; I'm telling you that you have got to do it." Then turning to his brother: "Get your hat and gun, Cliff, and tell Pompey to bring our horses. We're going to take this fellow to Willow Mills and let him face Bell Holderness with this wild tale of his."

Cliff left the room, and Lav spoke again to Dolly: "You may sit down."

"No, thank you," said Dolly. "I shoot better standing!"

"Shoot better! What do you mean by that?"

"I mean that when folks don't trust me, I don't trust them. You been wanting to kill Randy Ross. You've got the killing idea in your head, and you'll sure kill somebody if you don't look out."

"Father! Lav!" cried Zella, speaking for the first time. "Can't you see this young man is telling you the truth!"

"I can see that he has insulted me, and tried to blacken the name of the best friend we have," snapped Lav, "and I'm going to give him a chance to square it."

"You're going to crowd Bell Holderness, and get killed yourself," Zella almost choked.

"No, I'm not," Lav snapped. "I won't get killed at all right now, for I'm not going to turn my back to this friend of yours and Randy's. I told you to stay out of this mess. Whenever a woman breaks into a thing of this kind, she only makes more trouble for everybody. You were told to give Randy Ross up and forget him."

Zella made no reply. And neither did Dolly. Anywhere else on earth but where they were Lav would have answered to Dolly at once for his insinuation that the little puncher would shoot him in the back if he had a chance. By the time the horses were ready Dolly had cooled a bit. They went out to mount, where Dolly had left his own horse.

"Now get this," said Lav. "We're going to Willow Mills, and you are going to face Bell Holderness. There is but one of you and two of us. If you start anything, you may get one of us, but the other will get you. If you want to take a chance on a trade like that, it's up to you."

* * * *

Dolly was in real danger now, and, as usual in such cases, he began to banter them. His mission had failed. He wanted to kill Lav Tarleton for his insults, but he mustn't do it. As far as the two to one odds were concerned, that troubled him not at all. He was sure he could outshoot the two of them, but he was there to help Randy and Zella.

If he shot one or both of the Tarleton boys, it would be believed that Randy had sent him to do it. Besides that, he had no ill will toward Cliff. That young man had spoken but a few words to him, and they had been courteous ones. Cliff and Zella were alike, and evidently favored their mother. Lav was like the judge, but lacked the discretion of the judge's years.

"Maybe you fellows better take my gun," jeered Dolly. "You'll be safer, and I won't be afraid."

"We're safe enough," retorted Lav, "and you're safe enough with us, as long as you don't try to get too funny. You'll need your gun when you face Bell Holderness."

Dolly knew that was true. Unless he missed his guess, Bell knew enough by this time to make him desperate. Bell's only hope for safety lay in killing a few people, himself among others. These thoughts were in his mind as they stopped in front of the Cottonwood, dismounted, and went in. Two men, in chaps, spurs, and other garments of the range rider, were standing at the bar, drinking.

"Where's Bell?" Lav asked the bartender.

"I don't know. Him and French Clauson rode away from here together about night. I reckon they went to the H Bar."

"The H Bar! What business would Bell have there? He told me he had sold out all his interest over there and was not going back any more. Said he intended to build a home here at Willow Mills."

The bartender shrugged, and said nothing. He was trying to digest a message that had come to him over the grapevine a few minutes before. The man who had brought it stepped in the back door and slipped out again. Things were not going so well at the H Bar.

"'Scuse me, pardner," said one of the strangers. "If you mean Bell Holderness, I know where he is—or where he was about sundown. He was riding hell-for-leather for the H Bar, him and another fellow. Come take a drink, all you fellows," and the man threw a dollar on the bar. "Speakin' of the H Bar, they been having a party of some kind over there. We come from in on the Washita, and aimed to stay all night there, but it didn't look happy."

"What was the matter?" asked Lav.

"I don't know. There was about forty men there, some packin' one gun and some two, but nobody was talking. Some of 'em was diggin' holes in the ground, and four or five dead men lay in a wagon. It didn't look appetizing, nobody wanted to talk, we wasn't invited to stay, so we rode on."

"Was Bell there?"

"No, sir, he wasn't, but he was goin' there. We met him and the other fellow a mile this side of the H Bar, then about a mile the other side of the river we met Steve Holderness. He wasn't hurrying so much," and the man slowly poured another drink and swallowed it.

* * * *

"Did you talk to Steve?" asked the barkeep, apparently to get away from talking about Bell.

"Why, no, we didn't," the stranger said grimly. "Steve wasn't talking, either. He was right in the middle of the road, but couldn't get his feet on the ground. Looked like somebody had hung him out to dry. Everybody on yan side of the river has been expecting the H Bar to be took to a cleaning, but we didn't hear of it until we got there."

"You don't speak very respectfully of the dead," said Lav.

"Respectfully, hell, pardner! Don't nobody speak very respectfully of the Holderness gang over on the other side, whether they're dead or alive. The decent ranches, farther out in the Indian country, are getting ready to go in together and clean 'em up. Looks like if you was a cowman you'd know that."

"I'm not a cowman," returned Lav with dignity. "And I don't live on the other side."

"Oh, thataway. Well, I ain't talkin' secrets. They's cowmen on this side of the river, and they know that the H Bar is nothing but a hangout for thieves and killers. It's a reg'lar vest-pocket hell, and it's got to be cleaned. Somebody, I don't know who, has trimmed it some. They told us at the H Bar that Sam was dead. We saw Steve Holderness hanging up like a side of meat. That leaves only Bell to ramrod the outfit. I guess he was going home to lead his gang of killers against whoever it is that's riding them."

Dolly was very much awake now. What he had heard corroborated what the prisoner had told him at the crack in the smokehouse. The clans had gathered at the H Bar. Bell had seen the end of his plans unless he struck quickly. There was only one thing for him to do now, since so many of his plans had gone awry. That was to raid Silver Bend, kill Railroad and Randy, and as many more as he could, then let his killers scatter. With Steve dead there was no longer any one to hold lands in the Indian country. He had to act, and act with all possible speed.

Dolly had put all these things together in his mind as the stranger talked. He knew men, and he knew this stranger was telling the truth. He knew, too, that the man was not just an ordinary cow-puncher, for all he was clad like one.

"Say there's about forty at the H Bar?" he asked, as the man stopped talking and rolled a smoke.

"Yes, there was about that many in sight. Probably more scattered around. I knew some of 'em. Fellows there from several gangs. Some from Yellow Hills, some from the Arbuckle Mountains, and several other hangouts. Looked like a rustler's camp-meeting. Are you a cow hand?"

"Yes, sir. Name's Joe Runnels. Work for the Railroad outfit."

"Old Railroad Ross! You're working for a mighty square man. Thomas is my name, Alec Thomas. I run the T Stripe brand, in on the prairie between Red River and the Washita. I'm about an eighth Chickasaw, but nobody notices that, with these blue eyes of mine. Is it the Railroad that's working on the H Bar?"

"They been working on us some," replied Dolly cautiously.

"I see. Looks like you fellows been swapping work with 'em some. Take another drink, gents. We got to find a place to sleep."

As the men started out Thomas motioned Dolly to one side and whispered:

"I don't know who your friends are, but you better shake 'em and get back to the Railroad. Bell Holderness has got his gang bunched for something."

"That fellow's windy," sneered the bartender, as the two men went out and crossed to the little hotel.

"I know part of what he said is true," defended Dolly; and, turning to Lav: "Well, we ain't apt to see Bell to-night. What do you want to do?"

"I don't see anything we can do, except go back home."

"All right, let's ride."

* * * *

When they had almost reached the Tarleton house Dolly stopped them:

"Now see here, fellows. You talked pretty rough to me, but we'll forget that. You thought the Railroad outfit killed your brother. I've told you better, but you still don't believe it. You wouldn't believe Railroad, and you wouldn't believe Randy if he told you; but he'll never tell you anything. We can't see Bell Holderness, and he'd lie if we did see him. Anyway, I'd have killed him before he said anything, if we had met him. I can prove what I told you by witnesses that saw Bell shoot Ben in the back."

"Where are they?"

"Under lock and key, at the Railroad."

"We can't go there without—" and Lav stopped.

"Getting killed," Dolly finished for him. "Yes, you can. It takes some cold nerve, because the bottom is likely to be full of H Bar killers, but one of you can go there. There's just one man there that would hurt you, and he's asleep. That's Randy."

"Randy! Why would he hurt us?"

"Why wouldn't he? You've accused him of cold murder when he wasn't guilty. You've played in with the gang that murdered his brothers. You sent him word what would happen when you met him, and it'll happen—to you! But Randy ain't slept none for three nights, and he's dead to the world. It's up to you now. Either come with me and get proof from those men, or else put up your guns and stay out of this mess. Make up your mind, for I can't wait. I got business to attend to."

"I'll go with you," said Cliff calmly.

"Let's ride, then."

"Wait a minute," Lav protested. "What'll I tell father?"

"You ought to have more than you can tell him before morning, after what Thomas told you. You can tell him what Bell Holderness is, and ask why he hadn't found it out before now. You can tell him that what I told him was the truth, and Cliff will be back before morning, with proof of it. Dammit, tell anything. Tell him about the weather. Let's go, Cliff." And Dolly set spurs to his horse.

Perfect peace and quiet was over the Silver Bend, as they rode down from the prairie and took the trail to the Railroad. Dolly was wondering how long it would remain that way. They stopped at the corral. Dolly unsaddled his horse and turned it loose, then they stole through the darkness to the back of the log house where the prisoners were. A low call of his name brought Turk, or rather Walter, as Dolly knew him, to the wall.

"Now, tell this gentleman the story you told me about the killing of Ben Tarleton," said Dolly in a low tone.

Turk not only told it, but elaborated on it, and told it convincingly, averring again that he and his partner were making a sneak from the H Bar, because it was too tough, when they were caught.

"Satisfied now?" asked Dolly when they were back at the corral where Cliff had left his horse.

"Yes, more than satisfied. Zella told me some things that satisfied me that Bell was crooked and trying to play us for suckers, but I couldn't tell Lav and father. They won't reason in a case like this. They have to be shown. I came with you because I wanted to be able to show them."

"Good! Now, when you convince Lav and the judge, they are going to fly right around, like the arrow on the lightning rod when the wind changes. They'll want you and Lav to come romping down here to help Randy hang Bell Holderness. Don't do it. Some more water has got to run under the bridge before Randy is fit for you and Lav to meet. He may need help, but you can't help him now."

"Thank you," said Cliff, wringing Dolly's hand. "I won't come into Silver Bend unless I'm sure I can do some good." And he rode away into the night.

It was well after midnight, and Dolly was ready to call it a pretty full day. There was no sign of an attack on the ranch, and he needed sleep. He would have told Randy what he knew, or at least a part of it, but Randy needed sleep to put him in shape for what was likely to come on the morrow. A storm of disaster was brewing over Silver Bend that would have driven thoughts of sleep from Dolly's mind had he even dreamed of its terror.

CHAPTER XI

The Storm Strikes Silver Bend

Morning showed as peaceful a scene at Silver Bend as could have been found in all the long and winding reaches of that tawny river. The sun came up and gilded the silver of the young cottonwood trees. The dogwood was in bloom along with many other shrubs and wild flowers. A hundred mingled scents of sweetness were in the warm, damp air.

A great peace was over the world, but it was the calm before such a storm as Silver Bend had never known in all the more than thirty years that old Railroad Ross had struggled there. The elements that were to battle in that bottle and concoct a mess "unfit for human consumption," as Sankey had said at the outset, were rapidly fermenting for the mixture.

When Cliff returned home he found his father, Lav and Zella waiting together in the judge's bedroom.

"Well, what did you find out?" asked Lav.

"Just what I expected to find; that the young fellow who was here told the truth. There is no doubt that Bell Holderness shot Ben in the back, in order to make us think the Railroad outfit did it, and draw us into the quarrel on the side of the H Bar."

"Did you see Randy?" asked Zella.

"No; I was afraid to see him."

"Afraid!" rumbled the judge. "No Tarleton ever was afraid of any man."

"It wasn't the man I was afraid of. It was the result of what we had done. Lav sent Randy word that we would kill him on sight. I know what I'd do, and you know what you'd do, if a man sent you such a message. I don't want to kill Randy Ross, and I don't want him to kill me. One or the other will happen if he meets any of us before he is satisfied that we have learned the truth and changed our attitude toward him."

"Why, nonsense!" growled the judge. "If this trouble between the Railroad and the H Bar goes on, Randy ought to be glad to have you two boys on his side of the fight."

"That's true enough, but we can't go to him now. Dolly says he's as bitter against us as he is against the H Bar. That we all look alike to him."

"Why, I don't understand that attitude," said the judge.

"I do," declared Zella. "I'm to blame for part of it. You can't go to Randy, but I can. I'll crawl on hands and knees to him and beg him to forget what has happened."

"You'll do nothing of the kind," snapped Lav imperiously. "I've told you to keep out of this. No Tarleton is going to beg anybody to do anything. Go to bed. We'll decide what to do."

Zella went to her room, but not to bed. Gray dawn found her sitting at the window, looking down the river toward Silver Bend, as if she hoped to see Randy and what was happening to him. If she had seen him at that moment, she would have seen him still asleep. At sunrise she did see her two brothers mount and ride away toward Willow Mills.

"Where are the boys going?" she asked her father.

"To hunt Bell Holderness. He is a double traitor. He not only murdered my son, but accepted my hospitality and claimed to be my friend afterward. It would be a disgrace if my sons didn't hunt him down, since I am crippled and can't go myself."

If Lav and Cliff were to shoot it out with Bell that day, they'd have to go much farther than Willow Mills. Indeed, they meant to go farther than that, if they didn't find Bell in his usual haunts.

Quite unintentionally they were putting themselves where they could not help Randy.

Failing to find Bell in the little town, they took the road north toward the H Bar. The river was low, and they took the shallow ford and crossed to the other side, hoping to meet Bell as he came to town.

No man should say they were afraid. They didn't know it, but there was nothing to be afraid of in that neighborhood, unless it were the grim fruit that still hung from a limb over the road.

At daylight, even as Zella sat looking toward Silver Bend, Bell Holderness had left the H Bar with his men. Where they were going, the men didn't know, except that they were not going toward Willow Mills.

* * * *

Randy and his father finished breakfast and stepped out of the house to start the men on their day's work, when they met Dolly. "Mr. Ross, I got to talk to you and Randy some," Dolly remarked.

"What about?"

"Why, I went to Willow Mills last night, and—"

"Went to Willow Mills!" exclaimed Randy. "Didn't you know it was dangerous for any of our outfit to go there just now?"

"Yes, it was sorty shaky, but I found out something. Bell Holderness has gone back to the H Bar. He's got forty killers there with him. He knows Sam and Steve are dead, and he'll play his last card at once."

"What do you mean by his last card?" demanded Railroad.

"Why, he's got himself where he ain't safe as long as you and Randy are alive. He's desperate, at the last ditch, and he'll come here with his gang and kill you."

"How do you know all this?"

Dolly told him what Alec Thomas had said.

"I know Thomas," said Railroad. "He's a good, square man, and he knows the signs about such outfits as the H Bar. I never thought the Holderness boys would pull a thing like this, though. I knew it was a rough outfit, and I've heard some talk about 'em, but this is too rough."

"They're not the only rough ones," snapped Randy. "If they jump us in front, the Tarleton wing of their dirty outfit will stab us in the back."

"I don't think so," said Dolly.

Randy shot him a sharp glance, but said nothing.

"We'll keep the men all here at the ranch to-day, anyway," said Railroad. "I don't think they'll come across the river in the daytime, but our boys will need to be rested whenever they do come."

"I guess that's right," said Randy, thoughtfully. "No use in them riding the bend. They'll only get shot from the brush. Come on, Dolly. If they come into Silver Bend, they'll cross at the ford below the narrows. We'll go over there and watch."

Old Railroad stood watching them as they rode off. There went his last boy, riding into danger. It was the brave and manly thing to do, but he wished he could have gone himself, instead. Never had he seen such a change in any man as there had been in Randy, but he was too bitter, too venturesome. If the H Bar outfit did come that way, they'd get the boy sure.

"No work to-day, boys," Railroad told them. "Have the boys saddle and have their guns ready and loaded, but don't ride. Dolly says Bell Holderness is apt to come across, and jump us. He's got about forty killers. There's only twenty-two of us, without Dolly and Randy. They've gone to watch the ford. Don't any of the rest of you ride into the bottom. If they're in there, you'll just get shot from the brush, without having a chance. If they jump us here at the ranch, we'll have the advantage. Just get ready for anything that happens, but keep quiet."

Poor old Railroad. He had thought that battles of this sort were long past for him. He felt that this would be the last one if it came. He hoped it wouldn't come, but gamely oiled and loaded his guns. His old heart would beat rapidly for a moment, skip a beat, then slow down for a minute, keeping up an endless cycle of change in its working.

* * * *

Meantime, Randy and Dolly had ridden on to the river and ensconced themselves in a thicket, where they could watch the ford without being seen. Randy had not spoken since they left the ranch. Now he turned to Dolly and said:

"Where'd you go last night and what for?"

Dolly had been expecting that question, and dreading it. He was going to have to lie, or at least not tell all the truth, and he didn't like that sort of thing. He pulled himself together and plunged into the task.

"Why, I went to Willow Mills, like I told you."

"I know, but why? You didn't take a chance like that just for fun."

"No, I took it for you," and the earnestness of the little puncher's voice rang true. "I talked to that fellow Turk last night, and he told me what Bell would do in a showdown. I knew what we had done to the H Bar. I knew there was nobody but Bell left to ramrod the outfit. I wanted to know if Bell had gone to the H Bar, so I went to the Mills, and found out what I told you."

"All right. I never have caught you in a lie. I'll be sorry if Bell gets killed. I wanted him to marry Zella first."

"Randy, you oughtn't to be so bitter."

"Hell I oughtn't! Didn't she throw me cold? Hasn't Bell been there with her through all this mess? Ain't her brothers hunting me to kill me?"

Dolly wanted to tell him the Tarleton boys were no longer hunting him. He wanted to tell him that Zella was still true to him and suffering intensely for her part in the matter, but he didn't dare. Instead, he said:

"Randy, you're too hard on Miss Zella. I tell you she didn't understand—"

"And I want to tell you that she, or anybody else, will have one hell of a job making me understand that she didn't understand. I'm not a sucker any longer. Thanks to you, I'm a man now. I had to be mighty near killed to make me see sense. I had to lose about everything on earth that I loved, but thank God, the price shan't be paid in vain. I've still got my old daddy and mother, and I still have Silver Bend. It don't make much difference whether I come out of this mess alive or not, but if I do—"

Randy stopped. The thought was too bitter to express. It had to do with what he believed to be the unfaithfulness of Zella, and with his jealousy of Bell Holderness, which he refused to admit. At that moment, he thought there was no feeling in his heart for Zella, except to see her suffer in return for the pain she had given him.

Dolly offered no word. He was thinking again that he had tried to make a man, and made a monster. He had changed Randy from a shrinking boy to a fearless, even a desperate man. A man who could watch the quivering death throes of his enemies without a quiver. A man who could be a terrible enemy, even to a woman.

Looking down the river, as they watched the ford, Dolly was picturing in his mind the great bottle formed by Silver Bend. At the bottom of the bottle, and three miles north of the ranch house, the ground sloped up from the stream to a considerable height and formed a sort of plateau of a hundred yards in extent. There was no timber on it. The soil was loose sand.

In the middle of the plateau was a mound, on which grew an immense mustang grapevine. The vine was old and gnarled, supported by its own twisted stems, and a few stunted trees, it covered as much ground as a large house, and at a distance looked as much like a hay rick as anything else.

Dolly had eaten grapes at that vine many a time, squeezing the pulp from the grape into his mouth, without letting the skin, with its burning acid, touch his lips. He had no thought of any part that grapevine might play in the day's events. It was merely a vagary of his mind that it halted there a moment, in a mental journey from the bottom of the bottle to the ranch house.

The plateau, with its lone grapevine, was the sediment in the bottom of the bottle. To the south of the plateau, the ground sloped down sharply into a strip a quarter of a mile wide, filled with switch-cane and grass, with occasional trees in it. The strip was little higher than the river banks. Railroad Ross called it his winter horse pasture.

There was always green stuff there in the winter. It had not been burned over for several years, and was a mass of dead canes and grass, which protected the greenery under it in the winter. The swale ran across the bend from the river on the west to the river on the east. Beyond that, the ground rose sharply into thick timber that was on high ground and extended on to the prairie valley in which the ranch house stood.

* * * *

Dolly was trying to picture in his mind what might happen, and where it would most likely happen. He started when Randy said:

"Dolly, you've done a lot for me, but there's one more favor I want to ask. If the Holderness and Tarleton gang does come into Silver Bend, let me have Bell Holderness."

"All right," replied Dolly, absently. "They can come in most anywhere now. I never saw the river any lower. Listen! What's that?"

"Wind," replied Randy. "It's a spring norther. I noticed when it struck awhile ago."

They listened and the roaring increased.

"That ain't wind," said Dolly. "Look at the river!"

A wall of water ten feet high came rolling down the stream and thundered on by them.

"Huh! That closes the gate against the H Bar for awhile anyway," said Randy. "Most too early for a big head-rise, but that's big enough to stop them from crossing," and shaking his bridle reins, he led the way back toward the ranch.

They had almost reached the edge of the prairie at the round-up grounds, when Dolly said:

"I smell smoke! Looky how hazy it is," and then as they came out in the open: "Yonder it is! Somebody's fired the winter horse pasture. It'll burn the ranch!"

Randy's jaws set with a click, as his spurs went in and he thundered away toward the ranch house, with Dolly at his side. The men were mounting as they rode up.

"Come on, fellows!" shouted Randy. "We've got 'em in the open now. They'll have to fight. They can't get back across the river."

"Hold the deal!" roared Railroad, who had mounted his horse and had forgotten he had a heart. "They've set a trap for you if you go in there. Plenty of time to fire against that and save the house, if we have to. Wait till they make a move."

There was no long wait. Bell Holderness had come across with his forty killers. He didn't know yet that his retreat had been cut off by the high water. In his desperation he had but one thought. He was going to get Randy and old Railroad Ross.

When no one came from the ranch to fight the fire, he pushed on at the head of thirty of his men, intent on cleaning up the Railroad and burning the house. All he wanted was the land. The burned house would cover his crime. As they came out on the prairie, Randy whirled his horse and Dolly whirled with him.

"Come on, boys!" called Railroad. "They're ridin' straight into hell!" and dashed for the fray.

The battle was fought in the open this time. The hired killers had to fight or run. The Railroad riders had scores to settle and needed no urging. Four of them went from their saddle at the first crash of battle, but they were being terribly avenged. A dozen riderless horses of the invaders dashed across the prairie.

Bell's forces broke and scattered. He, with French Clauson, had been in the lead. Bullets had fairly rained around them, but they escaped. At last, seeing the battle lost, they turned and started for the bottom of the bottle, with their pursuers almost on them, for Randy and Dolly were riding with bloody spurs to overtake them.

The horse pasture was no longer burning. Instead, Bell and Clauson splashed through water almost to their saddle girths. They knew what had happened, and that retreat was cut off, but they didn't dare try to go back the other way now.

Bell knew some of his gang had gone the other way. He didn't know how many, but he cursed himself for not following them. His only hope was that his pursuers would founder in that quarter-mile morass that he had just passed.

* * * *

They didn't founder, but came doggedly on, though the water all but swam their horses the last few paces, and a strong current was setting across the bend.

"Now," said Randy, as they gained the plateau and their horses shook the water from their coats, "we'll have it out. Remember, you promised to let me have Bell. Let's go!"

Began then a battle to the death on that narrow plateau, which was now an island and gradually growing smaller.

Old Railroad and half a dozen of his men who had not been hurt in the battle came thundering down to the edge of the water, and stopped. They could see by the trees which they knew that they'd have to swim to reach the island. Across that strip of muddy water they could see the four men on the island. They watched, spellbound, as if they were looking at a play.

They heard the roar of shots, saw the island grow smaller and smaller, as the water rose around. They saw Randy's horse go down. Saw Randy rise on his elbow and fire at Bell, who was charging down on him. Saw Bell's horse fall, and saw him retreat to the other side of the little island, as Randy regained his feet and limped after him. A few yards away Dolly and Clauson met and shot it out. Both horses and both men went down.

Clauson lay still. Dolly struggled up, took a few steps toward Randy, and fell.

The final moment had come. With his back to the swirling water that had entrapped him, Bell made his last stand. He couldn't afford to miss this time. It was his last cartridge. He fired, but fired a second too late. Randy's bullet had found his heart, and Bell Holderness slipped into the swirling flood.

As if enraged at the pollution, the water, with a mighty surge, swept over the island, washing onto Dolly, who lay on the ground. Randy splashed to where the little puncher lay, and caught him up.

"Hit bad, Dolly?" he panted.

"No. Just in the leg, but we're going to get wet. I can't make it, but you got a chance. Swim for the tree."

"I won't leave you," declared Randy, splashing waist-deep toward the old grapevine.

Watching from the other side, Railroad and his men saw him gain the vine and push Dolly to safety, then, with the water already at his shoulders, pull himself up, and help Dolly to the highest point.

"Good God! Can't we do anything?" cried Railroad. "It'll go over 'em in a few minutes!"

"These little broncs couldn't swim it," said old Con, and the others knew it was true.

"I'd give everything I got for one big horse," declared Railroad, in a frenzy of anxiety.

"There's a chance for a trade," growled Con, as a powerful yellow horse came storming through the bottom toward them. It was old Judge Tarleton's big claybank saddle horse, and Zella was bestride him. It was a vicious brute of Arabian strain, deep-chested, and powerful of limb.

"Where's Randy?" she cried, as the horse skidded to a stop.

For answer they pointed to the grapevine and the two men clinging to the top of it.

"Let one of the boys have your horse," pleaded Railroad.

If she heard him, she didn't heed. In went her spurs. Openmouthed, the great beast reared, lunged, and went out of sight in the water until only Zella's head and shoulders could be seen. He rose and headed out into that swirling sea.

Railroad Ross watched with his heart in his mouth, and choked, as he cried: "What a woman!"

* * * *

They cheered as the great horse drifted against the up river side of the grapevine and stopped, but they couldn't hear what was being said, out there on that hopeless, swaying island, that was likely at any moment to uproot itself and float away.

"Take Dolly to a tree if you can," said Randy, grimly. "It won't make any difference about me."

"Oh, Randy!" cried Zella. "Please, please come on. There's a chance yet."

"No! We can't both go, and I won't leave Dolly."

"Go on, Randy, you damn fool!" stormed Dolly. "I don't count. Nobody'll miss me."

"No! I tell you I won't leave you!"

The big horse could just keep its head out of water and stand on the ground. Soon it would be swimming where it stood.

"Come on then, Dolly!" called the girl. "I'll take you to a tree and come back for Randy. Jump!"

Pushed by Randy, Dolly scrambled behind the saddle. At the same instant, Zella sprang out of it and landed on the grapevine.

"Go on, Dolly," she cried, "and God help you to win through."

"Zella!" Randy cried. "Don't make it any harder for me. Get back in that saddle."

"Not without you!"

"Then go on. I'll try—"

"You first. Catch a stirrup."

"No. I'll hold to the horse's tail."

"Go ahead."

He dropped into the flood, and ran his fingers into the mass of hair that floated on the water, just as Zella dropped to the saddle, and set the horse swimming toward shore. They had won about fifty feet when the watchers on the shore saw the old grapevine loose its moorings and float away.

They saw the logs and trash that swept over the spot, as a boom of drift gave way somewhere above it, but in tense silence, they watched the yellow head of that matchless horse, as he battled on with his double load. They saw the two heads above the water, as the horse submerged, all but his head, from time to time. Randy, they couldn't see, but never in all his life had Randy Ross wanted so much to live.

"God! I can't stand this!" said Sankey, as he threw off his boots, chaps, and hat. "Tie your ropes to me! I'm going in there."

Half a minute later, old Sankey pushed his mount into the water. No one there knew that it was not to save Zella and Randy that he breasted the flood on a small horse. It was to save that little blue-eyed puncher that he loved like a brother.

The watchers saw him win slowly on into the current, as they paid out the rope. Almost he had reached the trio, when the yellow horse went down. It came up, and went down again, came up, and fought feebly on.

"Don't let 'em tangle in the rope!" roared Railroad.

Sankey quit his spent pony, and with the rope in his teeth, battled for the bobbing yellow head. He gained it, and both he and the head went under, it seemed like for ages. Then Sankey floated clear and raised a hand. Railroad had hold of the rope, the yellow head was barely above the water. He felt a tug at the rope, as the gallant horse, spent to the last ounce of its strength, floated with the current.

"He made the rope fast to the bridle!" yelled Railroad. "Pull! Oh, damn you, pull!"

"Gimme the end of it," said old Con, and taking a half hitch on his saddle horn, set his horse to pulling.

A few minutes later, up to their armpits in the red water, Railroad and his men bore the rescued three to dry land. The great yellow horse scrambled out, stood for a moment quivering, and fell in his tracks, just as old Sankey gained the shore a hundred yards below them.

* * * *

It was late in the afternoon of the same day. The big yellow horse had revived, and had been taken to the Railroad pens, where he stood, gaunt and drawn, eating a light feed.

"He'll pull through now," opined Con, whose knowledge of horses was unquestioned.

"I hope he does," said Railroad. "He's worth about a million."

* * * *

On the gallery of the old ranch house, where they had been together since they had reached the house and changed to dry clothing, sat Randy and Zella. Neither of them had spoken for a long time.

"How did you ever happen to be in the bend, and riding that horse?" asked Randy.

"Why, I—Some people don't believe it, but when a woman loves a man as I have loved you, she knows when he is in danger. Lav and Cliff went away this morning, to hunt for Bell, they said. Pompey went off somewhere, and there was no one about the place. I got the feeling that you were in danger. It grew into a fear that Bell would talk Lav and Cliff into coming here to kill you. I decided to come and warn you. When I got to the barn there was no horse except father's big saddle horse, that no one but himself ever tried to handle. I don't know how I managed to put saddle and bridle on it, for it bit at me, and snorted terribly. I fought it, and mounted it, then I came like the wind over the prairie road.

"As I came into the bottom, I met two men who seemed to be flying for their lives. They checked, and one of them called: 'Don't go in there, lady. Hell's raging down there,' and they went storming on. If it was hell, and you were there, it was where I wanted to be, so I came on, and—you know the rest."

"Yes, I know the rest, Zella, up to now; and I'll do my best to make the rest more happy for you from now on. I'll never give you up again," and he took her in his arms.

* * * *

Out at the bunkshack, little Dolly was lying on a bunk, the doctor having dressed his wounds, along with those of several punchers who had been hurt in that first mad charge.

"What became of Turk and Bud?" he asked.

"Old man turned 'em loose," replied Sankey, who sat beside him. "Said Zella had proved what he wanted to prove by them, and that was that Zella and Randy would marry."

"Fine! Bully! I told you Randy was a thoroughbred, and all he needed was a little bustin'!"

"Yes," drawled Sankey, "but it took a woman to bust him. Lay down there and behave yourself. Randy has got him a side-partner now, and I'll need you as soon as you're able to ride."

"Workin' on the Railroad, workin' life away,
Workin' on the Railroad, for mighty little pay!"

"Shut up, Dolly, you make my head ache, and besides that you'll burst something, and start bleeding again."

www.ingramcontent.com/pod-product-compliance
Lightning Source LLC
Chambersburg PA
CBHW011438170626
46808CB00009B/3098